*Jason moved closer.*

He reached out and rested his warm hands gently on her arms. "And I am truly sorry for the way I treated you and how this whole ugly mess turned out." He pulled her an inch closer. "Will you ever be able to forgive me?"

"I told you five years ago I'd already forgiven you," she replied in a near whisper. *Just please don't ask me to forgive Tara.*

He searched over her face, his expression unreadable. "I don't believe you really have, and I'm not letting you leave this time until you do. I plan to make this up to you, Lauren."

"That won't be necess—"

"Yes, it is necessary," he said with conviction. Soft night sounds surrounded them, echoing as he slowly lowered his face to hers.

Lauren knew what was coming. Paralyzed, she let his lips brush lightly across hers, neither refusing nor responding.

"I will make this up to you, Lauren Wright. I promise!" With that, he bounded off the deck, down the wet steps, and to his car. "Nine-thirty! Be ready."

Lauren watched the road for several minutes after the sedan's taillights vanished into the darkness. Fear gripped at her heart. Jason's presence, his touch, his kiss—what was she to do? Her mind refused to believe, but her heart knew the awful truth. She was still in love with Jason Levitte!

**BETH LOUGHNER** is a regular columnist for the *Columbus Messenger Newspaper*, has contributed to various magazines, and has written three full-length dramas. She began writing in 1990 while enjoying her years as a stay-at-home mom. Beth also finds great excitement in her occupation as a registered nurse. Through her writing, she hopes to inspire others to find the true character of God and to encourage readers to apply these truths to their lives. Her husband and two children have made the beautiful state of Ohio their home. They love traveling to unusual places within the state and beyond its borders.

# Bay
# Island

*Beth Loughner*

Heartsong Presents

**A note from the Author:**
*I love to hear from my readers! You may correspond with me*
*by writing:*

> **Beth Loughner**
> **Author Relations**
> **PO Box 719**
> **Uhrichsville, OH 44683**

**ISBN 1-58660-933-5**

**BAY ISLAND**

Our mission is to publish and idstribute inspirational products offering exceptional value and biblical encouragement to the masses

All Scripture quotations are taken from the King James Version of the Bible.

All of the characters and events in this book are fictitious. Any resemblance to actual persons, living or dead, or to actual events is purely coincidental.

PRINTED IN THE U.S.A.

## one

Lauren Wright leaned heavily against the white painted rail, her hands tightly gripping its cool surface. Great belches of diesel fuel fumes reached to the upper deck of the ferry, giving her stomach an uneasy roll. Her eyes remained fixed ahead.

Bay Island loomed in the distance, drawing closer and closer as the boat plowed its way across Lake Erie. The once familiar trip now seemed out of place, distorted—suffocating. Five years' absence hadn't been enough.

A light breeze wafted across the warm waters, lifting the ends of her hair from her shoulders. Lauren gave a long-drawn-out sigh. A lifetime wouldn't be enough. A sense of dread overtook her again. She should never have come back. Tom Thurman had been wrong in asking her to come, wrong to think the past could be remedied.

The Bay-Line Ferry slowed, the steady noise of the throttle dropping to a hum as the boat edged toward the dock. Ferry workers scurried about, throwing thickly twined ropes to the waiting dockworkers in blue shirts. Reluctantly, Lauren followed the other passengers down the steep, narrow steps to the lower deck where her car was triple-parked in the gridlock of vehicles.

Skirting around the cars, she stopped suddenly, her eyes darting nervously toward the crowd waiting at the dock. What if. . . ? The thought hadn't occurred to her before. What if she were to meet Jason at the dock or on the road to Piney Point? What would she do? *No, no, that couldn't happen! He'd never recognize me—I've lost weight, I've changed, I'm more sophisticated now.* Still her heart pounded with agitation.

Lauren slipped quietly behind the wheel of her small sports car. Soon the line of cars ahead began crossing over the ramp, slapping the metal plate as it bobbed with the boat—clang, bam, clank, bam. Her car followed suit, and Lauren's hands were sweating as she steered the car down the main road.

Nothing much had changed at first glance. Beckette's Souvenir Shop had a bright new awning over the storefront, and the bike rental shop now had an enclosed building, but the simple store styles were still there. As she rounded the last corner, though, Lauren's eyes widened in surprise. The once familiar run-down Dairy Barn and Suzi's Boutique were gone. In their place was a newly designed shopping area. Levitte's Landing!

Lauren drew the car slowly to the curb as she gaped. Levitte's Landing! Jason Levitte's design. Jason's dream. He'd spoken for years about building the shops, designing a wharf-style area that would attract tourists. Slowly she counted the stores— eighteen, nineteen, twenty. It seemed so enormous—so crowded. People milled about the area, many watching as a small cruiser boat anchored itself alongside several other boats at the dock. Minutes ticked by as she continued to stare.

"You're parked illegally, Ma'am. I'm going to have to ask you to move."

Startled, Lauren took a calming breath before turning toward the voice. A tall, imposing figure of a police officer now stood by her door. "Oh, I'm sorry, I didn't—"

The officer leaned his tall frame down, alert blue eyes searching the back seat before returning his gaze to hers. A flicker of recognition crossed his face. "Lauren?" The sandy-haired officer moved closer, his tone less imposing now. "Is that you?"

Lauren shielded her eyes from the sun with one hand. "Yes," she answered hesitantly.

"You don't recognize me?" He laughed, his lopsided grin pulling to the right. "Larry—Larry Newkirk." He extended his hand through the open window.

"Larry—?" Lauren grasped his warm hand, her mind reaching back in time, dissolving into nothing. "I'm sorry—"

"I'll have to admit I'm a whole lot taller and more handsome now," the man said, his smile widening. "You might best remember me as the high-school senior who helped you with the Christmas play at church a few years back."

Lauren looked him full in the face, finally brightening with relief. "Of course, I remember you. And you're right; you are a whole lot taller."

"And more handsome, let's not forget," Larry added with a pleasant, low-rumbling laugh.

She offered him a small smile. "And more handsome."

"What brings you back to these parts?" he asked congenially. A split second was all it took before an uncomfortable look crossed his face. "I'm sorry! I didn't mean—"

"It's okay, Larry," Lauren assured, pressing a smile to her lips with effort. "I'm just here for a short vacation."

"At Piney Point?"

Lauren nodded, suddenly wishing she could end the conversation. "Well, I really—"

His brows drew together suddenly. "Does Jason know you're here?"

The question caught her off guard, tearing at her heart, the same heart she'd been convinced was healed. "No," she replied slowly. "And I'd really rather keep it that way—for right now."

"I understand," he answered, his voice taking on an odd quality. "If you need anything—"

"Thank you, but I'm sure I'll be fine." Lauren gave him a dismissing nod of her head, rolling up the window in one quick move. It took all she had to keep her foot off the accelerator until he'd moved. When he finally did, she maneuvered quickly into traffic.

It was too crazy, her coming back. Tom Thurman had convinced her to come back, convinced her there was no future for the two of them if she didn't. Oh, how she'd tried to tell him two weeks earlier that coming back to Bay Island would result in no good.

"I think you should go," Tom had said, sitting on the edge of her desk in the accounting department that day, munching an apple while she worked.

Lauren looked up from the billing statement she held and eyed him in disbelief. "You can't be serious." She glanced about the room to assure it was empty.

"They've all gone to lunch," Tom said intuitively, glancing at his watch. "Exactly where we should be right now."

"I'll be done in a minute."

"So?"

"So, what?"

Tom lowered the apple from his lips. "You know exactly what. I'll be through with seminary in less than three months and getting ready for missions training by Christmas. Where does that leave us?"

Lauren gently laid the billing statement aside and looked up at his strong profile. His coal-black hair shone in the florescent light above, and she gave him a whimsical look. Tom had been her rock for the past three years—loving, kind, gentle—real husband material. Yet, there was something. . .something that held her back. Not that she could put her finger on it exactly. Maybe it was a lack of romantic oomph that was causing her to hesitate.

"I don't know what God wants for us," Lauren finally said. "I don't even know what He wants for me."

"I know! That's exactly what I'm trying to tell you," Tom answered, his hand coming down over hers. "God has called me to missions, that much is clear. You haven't felt a call for anything in nearly five years."

"That's not fair, Tom," Lauren interrupted, her face reddening.

Tom lifted his hand, leaving coolness in its place. He swiped his hand over his face in a show of impatience. "It's very fair. You can't deny we have something very special together, and I've told you how much I love you, but you've got to know God's calling takes precedence over all that."

"I know."

"But if God has called me to missions and not you. . ."

Lauren gave him an apprehensive smile. "It'll all work out, Tom. A lot can happen in six months before your missions training." *Maybe God will change that direction. Being a pastor in the States would be nice. I could be a pastor's wife—but please, not a missionary. I don't want to go to Africa or Brazil.* She squashed those thoughts. "Maybe God will give me a desire to go into missions by then."

Tom shook his head. "Don't you get it? God's not going to call you anywhere, not until you've resolved the issue you left behind on Bay Island."

Lauren balked. "Bay Island has nothing to do with it."

"Doesn't it?" Tom asked, his voice giving rise to an unusual fervor. "You've never forgiven God for what happened on Bay Island, and you ran away from the problem before—"

Stunned, Lauren stood to her feet. "You weren't there! I didn't run away! I was pushed away. You didn't feel all the gawking eyes at church or hear all the whispering tongues." Unwanted tears welled in her eyes. Giving them an angry swipe, she continued. "I'd done nothing wrong, absolutely nothing."

Tom immediately pulled her into his arms. "I know. I know," he whispered gently into her hair. Slowly he pulled her back. "You and I both know you never sold those drawings. Most importantly, God knows."

Lauren shook her head miserably. "But he—they never believed me."

"You mean Jason, don't you? Why, you can't even say his name! You were once in love with Jason Levitte," Tom stated matter-of-factly.

"But—"

He laid a gentle finger on her lips. "Wait until I finish." A deep breath escaped. "No matter what you feel toward Jason right now, you were in love with him five years ago. You told me you'd forgiven him for falsely accusing you, even though you knew he still believed you'd sold him out."

"That's true!"

"That's nonsense!"

"How can you say that?"

"Because you're still angry with him, and you're still angry with God." Tom pulled her close again, his face pleading. "Haven't you ever wondered why you never get too deeply involved in any church ministries? You don't trust God anymore. He didn't make things right when you thought He should."

"I'm just cautious, that's all," Lauren answered, pulling herself away. "You're psychoanalyzing this whole thing too much. I've put Bay Island behind me. Please don't go dredging it up all over again. Bay Island has nothing to do with you and me."

"I wish it were so." Tom gave a sigh. "I want you to tell me, truthfully, if you really believe you've forgiven Jason, that you harbor no anger toward him, whatsoever. Tell me if Jason were to walk in here today, he'd be welcomed like any other brother in Christ."

"Tom, this is crazy," Lauren pleaded.

"No, it's not!" he retorted. "Let's get this out in the open." He leaned forward. "Tell me! Would you welcome Jason in here today?"

Lauren frowned. "Just because he's forgiven doesn't mean I ever want to see his face again."

"See! You're still angry with him," he said gently. "Just admit it!"

An answer didn't come to her right away. "He should have known better," Lauren finally said. "He should have known I'd never cheat him. Tara set him up—set me up—and he couldn't see it. Men can be so stupid!" She hadn't meant for the words to escape her mouth, and she immediately tried to snatch them back. "I didn't mean that."

"Yes, you did, Lauren."

Lauren hated it. She had meant it, every word of it. Yes, she was angry. Yes, God should have cleared the matter up by now. She'd given Him five years—five whole years.

"Lauren, I've prayed about this for months," he openly admitted. "And I really feel you need to talk this thing out with Jason. Then maybe we'll have a better sense of what God wants in your life."

"It's not fair, Tom. Going back to Bay Island could very well blow things up in my face. Nothing good could come of it." Lauren picked up the billing statement again, staring aimlessly at the figures. "Somehow, I know I'd—I'd lose you."

"The only way you can lose me is if you choose to do so." Tom's loving tone almost undid her. "And there's only one way to find out."

"There has to be another way," she reasoned, wrinkling the yellow paper with her grip.

"There's only one way. Go to Bay Island." Tom slowly took the paper from her grasp and ironed it out on his leg. "If not for yourself, then do it for me. I just know the answer's there."

"I can't just pick up and go," Lauren argued.

"Take a week's vacation," Tom suggested. "You have plenty of time coming, and your parents' cabin stands ready and waiting."

"I don't want to go."

"I know, but promise me you'll think about it."

"I'll think about it." *But I won't like it.*

# two

Soft pine needles blanketed the tree-lined road leading to Piney Point. Lauren purposely slowed the car to a crawl, breathing in the long-forgotten smells of pine and dewy foliage. An unexpected lump formed in her throat. Until now, she'd not realized how much she missed the place—the place she'd once considered a sanctuary.

The four-room cabin came into view as her car rounded the last turn, and Lauren immediately focused her attention to the large front deck. The screen door was propped wide open, its wood frame wedged tightly into place by a tipped lawn chair. A large box fan was busily sucking air from inside the door opening.

Lauren saw no one as she parked the car beside the cabin, the tires settling into old, shallow ruts cast perfectly to her wheelbase. Funny, after all these years. It was as if time had stood still—waiting.

Lauren stepped from the car, slowly taking in her surroundings. A strange ache settled over her. How could Piney Point feel so welcoming, yet uninviting, all within the same moment? Her thoughts were quickly interrupted by the loud echo of footsteps coming across the wooden deck.

"Come on over here, and let me get a good look at you," greeted a loud, familiar voice. The ample-sized woman strode down the deck steps toward her, a wide, toothy grin plastered on her face as she wiped her dusty hands on the blue apron tied around her thick waist. "Girl, it's so good to see you."

Lauren gave the woman a full grin, relief flowing through her as she happily let herself be enveloped in the woman's bear hug. "Tilly, it's good to see you too."

12

"I should say so, Girl," Tilly exclaimed, giving Lauren several welcoming swats between the shoulder blades with her big hand. Lauren nearly choked. Finally the woman forced Lauren back, eyeing her critically. "The years have been good to you, Lauren Wright; I'll have to give you that. And look at your hair. What have you done?"

"Had it cut and styled. It's been this way for quite some time," Lauren answered, fingering the curled ends. "Do you like it?"

"It looks mighty fine, it does," Tilly said, smoothing the ends brushing Lauren's shoulders. "Just never thought you'd ever let a pair of scissors near it."

"Yeah, well. . ." Lauren never finished the sentence. She knew what Tilly was thinking. Lauren's long hair had been the first thing to catch Jason Levitte's attention, and he'd never hidden the fact that he'd loved her flowing tresses. The hip-length hair had been the first thing to go after she left five years ago.

"And that outfit is really cute too."

"Thanks," Lauren murmured self-consciously, taking a look down at her denim jumper and white sneakers. The outfit was more casual than she usually allowed, but she'd determined to spend part of her vacation doing just that—vacationing.

"Your mom said you'd be coming today," Tilly went right on talking. "The cabin's clean and waiting for you. It's a mite stuffy, though. Don't know why your parents don't rent it out anymore, being high-peak season and all. But I guess that's none of my business." Tilly stopped for a moment's breather. "There's no sense standin' out here jawin', is there? Come in and look around."

Tilly led the way up the deck steps, and Lauren followed quietly behind. The swishing rhythm of Tilly's full skirt stopped when she paused long enough to set the fan aside from the doorway. They stepped inside.

"The phone should be hooked up sometime today, and the groceries your mom asked me to order are all put away. Even fixed that old finicky paddle fan," Tilly said, snapping the switch on the wall up and down to prove it.

"Tilly, I don't know what to say. The place looks great. I had no idea you'd be here getting the place ready. Mom never said anything."

"You know your mother," the older woman clucked, giving a heavy shrug of her shoulders. Lauren walked to the kitchen, one hand skipping lightly over the laminate surface. "How have you been, Tilly?"

"Finer than honey," Tilly answered, her eyes twinkling. "I couldn't be any finer now that you're back home."

Home! The word struck an odd chord in Lauren. Piney Point had always been a home away from home. For nearly a year, it had served as her only home. But her home was in Cincinnati, now. Her job was there. Tom was there.

Tilly Storm was the nearest neighbor to her parents' cabin, her own cabin only an eighth of a mile farther along Piney Point. Lauren's earliest recollection of Tilly was on her tenth birthday, the year her parents had bought the cabin. Tilly had fixed a big picnic lunch for her family, and Lauren thought the welcome basket was for her, for her birthday. No one had ever told her otherwise.

Over the years, Tilly became a permanent vacation fixture to Lauren, and she'd often dreamed of living on the island year-round as Tilly did. For one year that dream had come true—the year she'd met Jason.

"I'm assuming Jason still lives on the island," Lauren asked casually enough, belying the way her heart raced as she spoke his name aloud.

Tilly's smile dimmed. "Well, yes, he still lives on the island." There was caution in her voice. "He's moved to the north side, though. Built him a fine home at the inlet."

Lauren briefly turned her face from Tilly as she pretended to peruse the pantry cabinets. "At Muriel's Inlet?"

"Yep, that's the one. Built there about two years ago."

The blood nearly drained from Lauren's face. Muriel's Inlet! Surely Jason wouldn't have built the house he'd designed especially for her. Muriel's Inlet had been the intended location of their future home. True, they were never officially engaged, but they'd talked and dreamed of living at Muriel's Inlet in that house. What could he have been thinking? What if Jason had married? Could he have been so foolish as to marry Tara? She'd never bothered to let that horrible thought enter her head before.

"Has he married?" Lauren risked asking.

Tilly's dark eyes grew keen. "No, Girl, he hasn't." Her lips thinned out into a frown. "Don't reckon he ever will."

Lauren busied herself opening drawers, avoiding a reply. What could she say?

Tilly gave her a penetrating look. "I suppose you're here to get things settled between the two of you?" Silence. "I'd say it's about high time. It was bad business the way things were left. I'm glad you're going to work things out. I see now that neither one of you have been right since."

Lauren closed the last drawer more firmly than intended. "Don't go getting your hopes up, Tilly. I have someone else waiting back home." *My lifeline from this place—from Jason.*

This news drew a concerned wrinkle across Tilly's brow. "Your mom said—"

"I know what Mom said," Lauren interrupted with a sigh, remembering her mother's hopeful insights from an earlier conversation. "I'm not here to renew any relationships, just to set things straight. Then I plan to enjoy a few days of my vacation before going back home."

Tilly studied her. "I hope you can work things out, Girl. It's been a mighty shame the way things turned out."

Lauren smiled. Girl. Tilly had called her that ever since she could remember. The familiar sound of it had a comforting appeal. Then a frown slipped over her mouth. There was nothing really happy left on Bay Island, not anymore.

"Is Tara still hanging around?" Lauren finally asked. Tara! The name itself burned like fire under her skin. It was hard not to hate her. She'd been the one to deliberately deceive Jason, the one who single-handedly destroyed Lauren's reputation, effectively running her off the island.

Tilly seemed taken back by the question, and a look of disapproval crossed her face. "I know how she did you wrong, Lauren, but don't you think that's a bit—cruel?"

"In what way?" Lauren asked, astonished.

Tilly paused to study Lauren a moment. "You don't know?"

"Know what?"

Tilly seemed confused. "When's the last time you and Jason spoke?"

"The day I left here, five years ago," Lauren replied. "Why?"

"Then you didn't know Tara died last year?"

Lauren numbly shook her head, taking in the words. "Tara's dead?"

"You haven't talked with anyone from the island since you left?" Tilly asked again, as if the concept was too incredible to believe. "You never heard?"

Lauren pulled out one of the heavy maple chairs from the kitchen table and sat down. There was more unpleasant news ahead, she was sure of it. "I've pretty much avoided any Bay Island news over the years, Tilly, but evidently, something bigger than my own fall from grace has happened here since I left." The words sounded flippant and unfeeling, but Lauren truly didn't care.

"I'd just supposed Tara had called you."

"Called me?" Lauren asked in disbelief. "I should hardly think Tara would call me."

"She'd said she called you," Tilly answered, clearly disturbed by this new revelation.

"I promise you. I've not spoken to Tara or to Jason since the day I left here." Lauren's voice held an edge of sharpness.

"No offense to the dead, but since when did Tara's word carry any scrap of truth?"

Tilly shook her head vehemently. "Oh, Lauren, don't say such a thing."

"Tilly, I didn't come here to fight with Tara or Jason or anyone else. I've come to set things straight." Lauren's voice sobered. "I'm here to clear my name."

"But that's just it. Tara cleared your name two years ago."

The statement came like a bolt of lightning. Lauren swallowed quickly. "What are you talking about?"

Tilly blew out a lungful of air. "I'm gonna have to have coffee for this one," she announced, turning to the cupboard doors. Silence reigned as Tilly pulled out the filters, then the coffee canister, then the sugar bowl.

"Tilly," Lauren blurted out in exasperation. The wait was too much to endure. "You can talk while you fix the coffee. What did you mean about Tara clearing my name?"

"It'll be only a moment," Tilly answered, ignoring Lauren's mounting frustration. "Want some?" Tilly extended an empty coffee cup toward Lauren.

Lauren only shook her head, rubbing her temples impatiently. Why couldn't Tilly just get on with it?

"There," Tilly finally said, bringing over a brimming mug of coffee which threatened to spill over. Slowly she sank into the chair. "It's a rather long story. Where should I begin?"

"At the beginning," Lauren answered. "What's this business about Tara?"

Tilly seemed to have difficulty knowing where to start. "Well, after you left, the town was pretty much in an uproar over the drawings that were stolen and sold to that firm on the mainland. Of course, few of us knew the real truth about Tara then."

That was an understatement, Lauren thought spitefully. Even the church people had mentally convicted her without a trial. In all fairness, though, looking back, Lauren could see how they were used. Tara had orchestrated the deception with such methodic precision that the circumstantial evidence was hard to ignore.

"Things did settle down eventually," Tilly went on. "But then Tara was diagnosed with brain cancer about two years after you left. Guess the guilt was tearin' at her more than any of us knew. She even told her doctor that the cancer was a judgment from God for something she'd done in the past."

Lauren listened solemnly.

Tilly took a nervous sip of coffee. "Jason was by her side through all the radiation treatments and doctor visits. By then, they'd only given her three months—four tops. That's when she told Jason the truth about what happened, how she'd left the forged note on your desk, and how you'd delivered the plans to Williams and Tolbert. Tara even told him about all the little things she'd done to discredit you." She gave a weary shake of her head. "Jason was devastated—of course." Another shake of the head. "Oh, it was truly pathetic."

Lauren ignored the sympathetic inference. "You mean to tell me Jason's known for over two years of my innocence?" Lauren nearly exploded. Of all the nerve! Never once did he attempt to call and apologize for his brutish behavior. Not once! Lauren stood angrily to her feet.

"Sit down, Lauren," Tilly demanded sternly. "You have to listen to it all." When Lauren dropped back in the chair, sulking, Tilly continued. "Jason didn't make it easy on her, if that's what you're thinking. Tara wanted God's forgiveness, to become a Christian, but Jason knew from all the years of trying to reach her with the gospel, she'd have to come to God on His terms, not hers. I think Tara thought God would cure her of the cancer if she made things right."

Tilly folded her hands. "Jason just told her the truth. She was going to die no matter what she chose to do. There wasn't going to be any last-minute reprieves whether she got things right or not. She had to know it was her eternal soul at stake, not her physical life. Tara made a choice that day to follow Jesus."

Lauren didn't like what she was hearing. Anger simmered hot inside her soul as unholy thoughts revolved. Wasn't it just like Tara to squeak into heaven after all she'd done, after living the kind of life she had for twenty-five years?

"Tara went before the church that next Sunday and confessed, telling the whole nine yards of it," Tilly continued. "Jason told Tara she'd accused you falsely in public and that she'd have to exonerate you publicly. After she told the church, he demanded she talk with you."

"She never called," Lauren told her dryly.

Tilly looked thoughtful for a moment. "I thought for sure she had, but maybe she died before she could do it."

Lauren nearly snorted but thought better of it. "Things certainly aren't turning out as I'd expected," was all she would say.

"You need to talk with Jason," Tilly advised.

"Oh, we'll talk, all right," Lauren promised. "And I can't think of any better time to do it than today."

Tilly looked worried. "Better give him a chance to explain, Girl," she admonished. "Don't go at him with both barrels shooting."

Lauren paused a moment to calm her thoughts. Tilly was right! The golden opportunity was at hand, and she didn't want to muff it. Maybe this thing could be wrapped up nice and tidy, much earlier than expected. Somehow that didn't seem quite possible. Besides, Jason had a lot of explaining to do.

# three

A stiff wind blew through the open six-seater golf cart as it sped along the paved road skirting the shoreline. Lauren pressed her foot hard against the accelerator, running the electric engine for all its worth—all twenty-five miles per hour of it.

Jason! What could have possessed the man to go to such great lengths to finally clear her name, yet leave her to lie in its poison for no cause? What good could he have hoped to accomplish? And the house! How would she react if Jason had actually built her dream house—possibly for another woman? It wouldn't be long until she'd find out. Muriel's Inlet was less than a mile away, and she'd have plenty of time to catch a peek at the house before finding her way to Jason's office. He'd be at his office, of that she was sure. His Saturday hours hadn't changed according to Tilly. He'd been a workaholic then and was most assuredly one now.

That Tilly had thoughtfully recharged the battery of her parents' cart was so appreciated. Lauren had always loved puttering about the island in the thing, especially when the weather was as glorious as it was that day. If only her mission were as pleasant.

Lauren drew in a deep breath. An earthy moisture was coming across the lake, mixing itself with the abundance of island honeysuckle. There was a rainstorm coming. Lauren could smell it. Rhythmic waves lapped loudly at the huge rocks as she passed an open stretch of shore. Several other carts passed by in the opposite direction, each driver giving an easy wave of greeting. Lauren smiled and waved back absentmindedly, her thoughts still churning.

Jason! She'd rehearsed their meeting so many times in her

head it was quickly becoming a blur. No introductory statement seemed right. *Hello, Jason, remember me?* Or maybe the direct approach. *Jason, we need to talk. What were you thinking? How could you have kept silent?*

Would Jason even have an explanation for his behavior? He'd been so sure of her guilt five years before. That fact alone hurt more than anything. The memory of that ugly day was forever etched in her mind, a memory that now circled like a hungry vulture.

"Jason," Lauren had called to him when he'd entered the office that afternoon. "We need to go over the Ross account. Do you have time now or—"

Jason had stopped at his open office door, a manila envelope tucked under his arm. Icy gray eyes fixed on hers, and she instinctively stopped midsentence.

He was quiet for several long seconds. "I want to see you in my office right now. You won't need the Ross report," he said, his voice low and menacing.

Lauren became uncomfortably aware of the sudden tension in the room. Only two other workers, Tara and a receptionist, were within easy earshot, and they seemed to be holding their breath in wait. Never before had Jason used that tone with her.

Lauren felt her cheeks go warm, but she confidently rose from her chair and walked the length of the hallway to his office before pausing at his door.

"Close it behind you!"

Still Lauren said nothing, then quietly closed the door. He faced her from behind the desk, his large frame hovering, waiting. His features, too finely chiseled to be truly handsome, now seemed carved out of stone. His square, determined jaw was clenched. Jason was furious. That much she could tell. But at what—or whom? Jason was never one to rant or rave, or to raise his voice, yet she felt his anger, radiating as it was now.

"Sit down!"

"I'd rather stand, thank you," Lauren replied, her defenses

rallying. She bravely neared his desk. There was no doubt now. She was the target of his anger, although she could conceive of no reason why she should be. Something serious was at stake. "What's wrong, Jason?"

His eyes narrowed dangerously. "You tell me," his harsh voice demanded as he suddenly withdrew the contents of the manila envelope. Several eight-by-ten glossies slid haphazardly across his desk as he tossed them toward her.

Lauren let her eyes wander to the black-and-white prints. Gingerly, she picked one up and then another. "What are these?" she asked, studying the office building which was focused into view on the prints. A small gold sports car in the right-hand corner caught her eye. Her car!

Jason didn't answer, but extended yet another photo toward her. Lauren silently took it. Her own image peered back into the camera's zoomed lens, apparently as she was leaving the office building.

"I don't understand, Jason," Lauren spoke, desperately keeping her voice calm. "Why do you have these pictures?" She fingered through several others. It was obvious the photos had been taken the previous afternoon while she was on an errand delivering a tube of drawings to the mainland.

"I had you followed."

"Followed?" Lauren eyed him indignantly. "Jason, have you gone stark-raving mad? Why would you have me followed?"

His smile wasn't a pleasant one. His shoulders straightened beneath his checked shirt and blue tie. "I'd hoped it wasn't true, Lauren, but these pictures don't lie." He ran his hand impatiently through his blond hair. "Why would you do this to me?"

"Do what to you?" Lauren was reaching the point of exasperation. "I delivered the drawings as you asked. Was there a problem with the drawings?"

"I asked you to?" He spoke brusquely, disregarding her question. "That's a lie."

Lauren flinched at his venomous tone, then forced her shoulders back in a show of courage. "Yes, you! You left the message on my desk asking me to deliver the tube of drawings."

"You stole those drawings, Lauren," Jason accused. "You stole those drawings and sold them to Phil Tolbert."

"Stole your drawings!" A hollow laugh erupted. "You can't be serious, Jason."

"You're about to see how serious I can be," Jason threatened.

Lauren stared in disbelief. Was this the same man she'd fallen in love with over the past year, the reasonable man with whom she'd dreamed over their perfect house, the man who'd actually sketched the designs lovingly into form?

"I have the proof, Lauren, if you'd care to look at it."

"Proof?"

Jason silently opened the top drawer of his desk and handed her a business-size envelope. Lauren withdrew the contents.

"These are my bank records," she breathed incredulously, looking up at Jason. "What are you doing with these? And how did you get them?" Her eyes fell back to the copied statements in her hand, settling on the account balance highlighted in yellow. Twenty thousand! Never in her life had she accumulated that much money.

"Was it worth the money?" His taunting words shot through her.

"Jason, I swear, I have no idea—"

"I do," Jason interrupted, stabbing his finger at another photo of her and Phil Tolbert. "What I don't understand is why. Did you need the money? You know I'd have given you the shirt off my back if you'd just asked. Did you think I'd never figure out what you'd done until everything was drained, including my business?"

Suddenly Lauren knew. A tiny light began to glow. Insignificant events, which meant nothing before, meant everything now. There was the day her purse was missing from work. Frantically, she'd searched, only to have the purse show up a half hour later in the same spot where she'd left it. And what about the mysterious blips from the computer indicating her password commands were malfunctioning, or the funny feeling she'd had when Jason left the message for her, not Tara, to deliver plans to Phil Tolbert?

Tara! It had to be her. Lauren had known there would be trouble from the first day she'd laid eyes on her. Tara had her hopes set on Jason and although she was only twenty, ten years his junior, she wanted no one encroaching on her territory. Jason was blind to the facts, that much was obvious. Lauren's attempt at pointing out that certainty to him had met with an adamant denial.

"She's only a kid in need of the Lord," he'd said.

Tara had worked as Jason's assistant for nearly a year before he'd met Lauren on the island during her vacation. Jason and Lauren had built a long-distance, occasional-visit relationship over that year, finally resulting in her taking permanent residence on the island, working as his accountant. Tara hadn't liked the intrusion, but appeared satisfied with the current attention Jason had given her in his many attempts to reach her with the gospel. But Lauren saw through Tara's facade easily. Tara had no real interest in spiritual matters, but she was more than willing to string along a willing Jason—just long enough to keep his attention and time focused her way.

But would Tara stoop to such depths to remove Lauren? An uneasy suspicion settled the question. Yes! Yes, she would!

"There has to be an explanation, Jason," Lauren pleaded.

"And what would that be?"

Lauren took a deep breath, suddenly afraid. He'd never believe Tara was capable of setting her up. He was much too blind concerning the young girl. But Lauren had no choice except to attempt reasoning with the man. "It's obvious that I've been framed—there's no other explanation. I would never hurt you, Jason, you know that. How could you even think me capable of doing something like that?"

Slowly he walked around the desk until he stood before her. "How, indeed?" He gave her an odd, level look. "And just who then, Miss Nancy Drew, do you think is capable of doing such a thing?"

His arrogant tone wound the tension one level higher. There would be no reasoning with Jason, not at that moment, and his cavalier acceptance of her guilt irked her. "If you were so clever," she was stung to retort, "you'd know."

He gave her a smoldering look but said nothing for several seconds. Instead, he gathered the glossy photos and stuffed them back into the folder. "If I'd been so clever, I'd never have let myself in for this mess, Lauren."

The utter contempt in his voice shook her. It was coming to her very quickly that she was engaged in a battle that might never be won.

"I want you to clear out your desk," he demanded.

Lauren knew in that moment the final irrevocable act would take place. He was letting her go, detaching her from his work and most of all, his heart. She stared stonily at him.

"It's best to keep this little affair quiet, don't you think?" he went on. "I have no desire to press charges, but I do want the money back."

"The money?" Lauren blinked. "But, Jason, I have no idea where that money came from or who it belongs to."

"I know who it belongs to. It's mine, and I want the money back!"

Lauren glared defiantly up at him. "You're impossible." She leaned close to his face, anger surging through her veins. "I told you once a long time ago we should have never been paired, that dating someone who's obsessed with moving up the financial ladder of success was a bad idea. People with money think about only one thing: protecting themselves and their assets. Didn't I tell you that? You're so suspicious of everyone's motives, you can't even think straight enough to see the obvious." Lauren had to fight to keep her voice even. "I'll leave your precious little office, Mr. Big Shot, but if you want the money, you'll have to take it the same way it got there—

without my help or my knowledge."

Lauren didn't wait for a response, but turned on her heel and quietly left his office. Ignoring the subtle stares of the office staff as they returned from lunch, Lauren efficiently emptied her desk of every personal possession. Tara was conspicuously absent which boiled her blood another ten degrees higher. With her chin held high, Lauren gave a final glance back at her desk before exiting the front doors.

It wasn't until two months later that Jason spoke again with Lauren—the day she'd left the island for good.

"You're leaving?" Jason asked coolly, leaning on the hood of his black sedan as he watched Lauren pack the trunk of her car.

"It would seem so," Lauren answered with a hard edge to her voice. "Is there something you wanted, or did you just come by to gloat?" Why had he shown up? She didn't need any more grief. The faster she packed and left Bay Island, the better.

He didn't answer right away. "No, I just thought you might have something to say to me before you left."

Her gaze raked over his face. All her pent-up frustration of the past weeks, all the resentment she felt toward Jason and her fellow church members, threatened to blow. The news about her alleged wrongdoing had spread fast across the island and through their church, thanks to Tara. It hadn't surprised Lauren. But she was surprised and dismayed at her church family who seemed even less forgiving than the rest.

Lauren swallowed hard, fighting back the sting of tears as she thought about the dwindling number of students in her junior Sunday school class. Parents had pulled their children from her class when they'd heard. The glances, the whispering—it was too much. It was time to leave the island, her church—and Jason. It was the only way. She'd tried to brave it out, hoping against hope her name would be cleared. But it hadn't. Why was God allowing this miscarriage of justice?

"Let me help you," Jason said, stepping forward to take the

heavy suitcase she was about to heave into the trunk.

Lauren quickly tugged it out of his reach. "No, thank you. I can get everything myself, if you don't mind."

Jason clenched his teeth, and she saw his jaw muscles twitch. "I'm trying to be as understanding as possible."

"It's a bit too late for that," Lauren retorted. The heavy bag landed with a thud in the trunk. She stopped and looked at him. "But I do have something for you."

He looked puzzled as Lauren opened the car door and scooped her purse out from the front seat. Quietly she searched through the contents.

"Here!" Lauren handed him a dark blue checkbook. "I've taken out what's mine. Do what you want with the rest of it." Why he'd never claimed the money before now was beyond her.

Jason accepted the book. "I've figured out where the twenty grand came from," he told her, then paused. Lauren ignored the bait and piled in another bag. "The money was taken from the supply fund in the form of a check made payable to cash," he went on. Still, Lauren packed. "Aren't you at all curious how I've tracked it?"

"Not at all," Lauren answered, slamming the trunk lid shut. "Matter of fact, I don't much care what you've found or haven't found. The bottom line is you think I ripped you off, and that's all that matters in the long run, isn't it?" She swung around to face him. "But I will tell you one thing. The truth has a way of coming out. Oh, it may take another week or a month or maybe even a year, but the truth will eventually come out, Jason. When it does, don't bother calling to apologize. It'll be too late for anything to be done about it by then."

"I think we both know the truth." His tone was disconcerting, as was the expression in his eyes. "I'd have forgiven you if you'd just admitted what you'd done."

Lauren laughed. "On the contrary, I have already forgiven

you for the false accusation. I can only ask that God will do the same." *That should heap some self-righteous coals on your head.*

Jason slowly shook his head, an action Lauren interpreted as pity. "Where will you go?"

"Why should it matter?"

"I still care about what happens to you."

Lauren opened the door of her car, tossing her long French braid to one side as she slipped inside. "That's mighty neighborly of you," she retorted, starting the car. "But you lost that privilege the day you accused me of the unthinkable."

With that, Lauren propelled the car forward, never looking back, never seeing Jason's expression.

## *four*

As soon as Lauren rounded the bend at Muriel's Inlet, she saw it. The beautiful house stood regal and tall, a commanding sight at the top of the sloped acreage. Lauren let the cart coast to a stop on the graveled shoulder. Looking up, she merely shook her head in disbelief. *Jason, how could you?* The coloring, the windows, the decorative trim—everything was exactly as she'd dreamed, right down to the white Adirondack chairs gracing the wide wraparound porch.

Lauren alighted from the cart to get a better look. Every door and window was shut tight, an emptiness seeming to surround the house. The driveway was vacant. No one was there to keep Lauren from openly gazing at the structure.

The tall Cinderella-type tower immediately caught her attention. It jutted off the second floor with a large stained glass window on one side and a small balcony facing the lake on the other. Puzzled, she drew her brows together. The tower had never been part of the original plans. Yet she couldn't deny the beauty it gave the home, the fairy-tale wonder it evoked.

Her gaze wandered across the perfectly landscaped lawn, which extended well out of view. It was hard to believe Jason had actually forged ahead with the building plans. And for what? The large house was much too big for him alone. Another thought stirred. Maybe he wasn't alone. Tilly said he hadn't married, but that didn't mean there wasn't someone special in his life, a future Mrs. Levitte. Could he be so callous as to build Lauren's dream house for another woman?

She looked beyond the gazebo in the side yard, the white cast iron tea table set inside giving it picturesque perfection. Everything looked perfectly in place. It was as if life on the island had never changed or paused for a moment because of her departure. Didn't those on the island realize the sacrifice she'd been unjustly asked to pay. . .how those events shaped her life, nearly unraveling her faith in God?

Several minutes lapsed before Lauren settled herself back into the cart, her melancholy mood causing a long, deep sigh as she slowly turned the cart around. She wasn't ready to face Jason, not just yet. Things were happening too fast. There were too many things defying logic or understanding. Thoughtfully she drove one block down to the public access path which led to the rocky shore. The familiar rock structures were the same, a welcoming sight she'd enjoyed years ago. Slowly she stretched her frame from the cart and walked to the shore. Lauren was pleased she could still climb the steep, pitted rocks surefootedly.

The wind tugged at the hem of her dress as she gingerly stepped from one stone to another. There was a definite smell of rain now, and the choppy waves indicated the storm would present itself in only a few hours. Lauren eyed the point, a large rock fifty feet into the deep water. Cautiously she made her way across, jumping rock to rock, careful to keep her white shoes dry.

The view was spectacular as always. From the point, one could clearly see Muriel's Lighthouse at the tip of the shoreline. How many times had she sat on that rock, looking, taking in the sounds of the water and screeching seagulls?

Lauren turned around and looked past the short cliff where Jason lived. The house was hidden from view, everything except for the tower, which also enjoyed an unobstructed view of the lighthouse. She turned back to the water, mesmerized. Minutes ticked by. The wind picked up, throwing water higher, an occasional gust causing the water to kiss at her feet. Eyes closed, she drank in the smells and sounds.

"Lady!" A man's urgent voice interrupted the tranquility.

Lauren turned slowly to face the distraction, her heart

sinking straight to her sneakers when she caught sight of Jason making his way down the rocky cliff. His unmistakable figure stopped halfway down when he noticed her undivided attention.

"It's not safe out there," he yelled against the wind. "You'd better get back to shore." He waved for her to come in.

It was apparent he hadn't recognized her. Lauren didn't move, but continued to stare at him, and he began his descent again. His blond head bobbed several times from the rough terrain. His footing slipped on the loose stones, but he quickly righted himself.

Jason finally made it to the shoreline, and Lauren wondered if he'd recognize her now with the distance closing between them.

"You need to come back," Jason yelled again, concern still vibrating in his voice. "Are you stuck out there?" Lauren's relative calm must have given him cause to worry for his forehead wrinkled in deliberation, his gaze fixed on hers for several seconds. Then he seemed to grow impatient with her silence. "Why won't you answer?"

Lauren watched as Jason suddenly began making his way across the same stones she herself had traveled. His long legs brought him farther into the waters, drawing him closer and closer. Unnervingly, his eyes never left her. Lauren scrutinized his expression, wondering if he'd yet made the connection. She couldn't tell. It wasn't until he'd safely reached the point, when he stood only five feet from her, his realization became quite evident.

Their gazes locked for several moments. Finally, he broke the silence.

"So, you've come back." Although his tone was gentle, it was flat and oddly insulting. The wind ruffled his loose, pullover shirt as he folded his arms across his chest, waiting.

"Yes!" Lauren finally tore her gaze from the gray eyes fixed on her. She let her eyes roam over the churning waves, desperately trying to collect her thoughts. They weren't supposed to meet like this, unprepared and by chance. She could barely catch her breath, let alone conjure up her earlier anger toward him, the anger he deserved. The sight of him completely unraveled her.

"Why didn't you answer? I thought you were some loon trying to commit suicide." His tone let her know he was annoyed.

Lauren let her gaze wander slowly back to his face, tipping her chin up high. "Guess I couldn't resist the temptation of climbing the point just one more time." She drew in a breath. "I didn't want to be disturbed."

"It's my business to disturb those who trespass on the point," Jason declared with authority. "This is private property now."

She caught the full meaning of his words. "I suppose that shouldn't surprise me. Everything at Bay Island has changed." Her voice was deceptively calm, and she applauded herself.

His gaze roved over her, settling on her hair as it whipped about her face in the wind. "You've changed quite a bit, yourself. I see you've cut your hair."

There was no sense asking what he thought about the shortened version; Lauren already knew, and she suspected he knew why she'd had her beautiful mane cut. She also knew he'd noticed her new slender figure, but the "new her" gave Lauren no pleasure at the moment. "A lot of things have changed in the past five years." She tilted her head. "How have you been, Jason?"

His face remained expressionless. "I've managed. And you?"

Jason wasn't making their unexpected reunion any easier. And it was obvious he was nowhere near being the least bit repentant about his past actions against her. Instead, he seemed angry, as if expecting something from her.

Lauren shrugged. "I suppose I've done all right—all things considered."

His jaw muscles twitched. "You seem to have done exceptionally well, if you ask me." He shifted his six-foot frame.

"And to what do we owe this unexpected visit, Lauren?"

This was Lauren's chance to let the years of rehearsed words spill out, to live the scenes she'd evoked in her mind, the ones in which she triumphed. Five years of the drill should have prepared her better. Instead, she felt empty, drained. Thoughts circled aimlessly, unable to take form.

A sudden gust of wind pushed against her, and Lauren scampered backward, nearly losing her footing. Jason's hand shot out, locking on her arm as water lapped across the tops of their shoes.

Lauren shrugged off his grasp. "I'm okay!"

Jason seemed irritated by the interruption. He pointed toward the incoming dark clouds. "The clouds are starting to build to the north," he said. "We'd better head back to the shore before we both get swept out to sea."

Jason threw her an expectant glance before hopping down to the next rock. Lauren grudgingly followed his lead. Twice he grasped her hand to help her across the more treacherous areas. Lauren's hands burned at his touch. Why did he still affect her to the point of craziness? Something was so disjointed about his behavior, and it bothered her terribly. It was as if nothing had changed, as if he was still angry with her. He hadn't wanted her to come back. What was wrong with the man? He owed her an explanation and at the very least, one or two sheepish looks of embarrassment. But he'd given her none of that, none at all.

Lauren stopped suddenly, and Jason threw her a quick glance.

"What's the matter?" he asked impatiently.

"What's the matter?" she echoed sarcastically. "For starters, your attitude. I'll never understand you, Jason Levitte!"

"Join the crowd," he remarked flippantly as water licked at his shoes again. "But do you think we could discuss this on dry land? We'll both be soaked if we wait here for the storm to push in any further."

Lauren moved reluctantly, caring less about getting wet than his attitude. He was as commanding as ever, even to the point of protectiveness, but she wasn't fooled into thinking he cared one iota about her. It was just his way, regardless of what he liked or disliked. Even in his contempt for her five years earlier, he'd tried his best to extend a way out for her, misguided as it might have been.

"We'll go to the house," Jason said as soon as they reached the shoreline. "We're way overdue for a long, hard talk, and I definitely have a few things to say."

Lauren eyed the visible tower. "I'd rather talk right here, if you don't mind." She had no desire to see the house which held her wasted dreams, to possibly see another woman's handiwork displayed.

Jason followed her gaze, and Lauren thought he'd paled for a moment, but he gave no indication when he spoke. "I don't plan on standing out here with the storm bearing down on us, nor do I have any intention of letting you go this time. At least not until we've properly hashed this thing out. It's been too many years coming. Now, are you coming to the house or not?"

"No," Lauren told him firmly. "I'm not going up to your house. Do you think I'm blind? Did you think I wouldn't recognize it? You built my house, Jason, the one I invented and dreamed of." She was angry and hurt by his offhanded manner. Didn't he know the house represented his ability to go on without her, the ability to disregard her memory as if she were nothing? "It's cruel, Jason. Did you do it for spite, hoping to see the day I'd view it as a memorial to what could have been?"

Jason said nothing for a moment. "No. That's not why I built it."

"Then why, Jason?" she demanded. "Did you take a leave of your senses? Why did you waste your time building this house when you should have been trying to find me? I deserved the courtesy of being told I'd been cleared." The hurt in her gut cut like a knife. "I couldn't have been that hard to find."

"No, you weren't hard to find at all," Jason said sharply. "Twenty-five thirty-six Brandon Parkway, Cincinnati, Ohio. How could I forget? It's blazed into my memory."

Lauren froze, her body, her mind, turning to stone. "You knew? You've known all this time where I lived, and you never thought to call me up and tell me? You couldn't have phoned and said, 'Hey, Lauren, the truth is out now. Guess I made a little mistake.'?" Frustrated anger seared at her throat. "Didn't you think I deserved that, Jason Levitte? It was heartless and inhumane to let me go on thinking people still hated and despised me."

"They never hated or despised you," Jason snapped. "I know it was rough—"

"Rough!" she nearly spat. How dare he! "You want to hear what rough is?" But her words stopped cold. No, she wasn't about to let him gloat over her misfortunes, to let him know how she'd left her faith until Tom Thurman had nurtured her back to spiritual health again. Tom! Why had he ever insisted she come? Where was he now when she truly needed him?

"Let's speak about being heartless and inhumane," he demanded back, his voice brusque. "Let's talk about Tara and her feelings."

Lauren couldn't believe the man's audacity. "Tara and her feelings?" she asked incredulously. "What about mine? Or have you forgotten who the real victim of this charade is?"

"In the end, we were all victims, Lauren." His eyes challenged her to disagree.

"Oh, yes," Lauren said tartly, throwing all caution to the wind. "I've heard about Tara's so-called conversion. Pardon me if I'm a bit skeptical."

He watched her with narrowed eyes. "You've changed, Lauren," he finally said. "And I must say, cynicism doesn't become you. Tara did her best to explain things to you and ask your forgiveness. But you'd have none of it, would you?"

Lauren forced herself to meet his gaze. "Have none of what?"

"Tara's apology, of course." He eyed her suspiciously. "Don't play innocent."

This was the second time Lauren had heard of the mysterious conversation she'd supposedly had with Tara. "I've not spoken with Tara since I left here," she challenged.

"That's impossible. I was in the room when Tara called." His eyes narrowed. "I heard her half of the conversation, and it wasn't pretty, I can tell you."

There they were again! Back to square one—him accusing, her denying.

"I'm telling you, Tara never called me," Lauren protested angrily. "Choose what you want to believe, but at least let your memory serve you right. We went through a similar scene like this five years ago. I don't plan on going there again. Just remember who told you the truth then."

The fierce fire in his eyes dimmed as he rubbed his hand thoughtfully across his jaw. "You're right. I don't understand what's going on." He gave an exaggerated sigh. "And I don't plan to make the same mistake twice."

The loud bark erupted suddenly from atop the cliff. Jason jerked his attention to the offending noise. A black Labrador retriever peeked over the cliff's edge, resounding another bark before sniffing at the air toward them.

"Stay up there, Butch," Jason commanded the dog.

A woman immediately joined the dog at the cliff, glancing quizzically between Jason and Lauren. Her petite form struggled slightly with the wind, her long black hair fanning out behind her.

The woman called to Jason uncertainly. "You have a call from Levitte's Landing, and they say it's urgent." She looked back at Lauren, caution in her eyes. "Do you want me to take a message or can you come?"

Lauren watched the indecision in Jason's eyes. "Go ahead, Jason," she told him. It figured! Finally they'd reached a point in their conversation where it was beginning to go somewhere, and his work interfered—again. Why didn't that surprise her? How many times had their dates and plans been interrupted by business?

"Tell them to hold on. I'll be up in a minute," he answered the woman abruptly. His focus returned to Lauren as the woman and dog turned away. "I'm sorry, but I really do have to take the call." Still he didn't move.

"I understand." She didn't.

"No, you don't," he replied without rancor. "You never did understand the demands of my work." He looked back to the cliff. "It looks as if now is not the best time for us to go up to the house, anyway." He thought a moment. "Are you at Piney Point?"

Lauren nodded.

He consulted his watch. "Give me two hours, and I'll be there. We'll get this whole mess straightened out." She felt him move closer to her. "Temporary truce?"

She was silent, thinking. "Temporary truce," she finally agreed. Very temporary.

He nodded his head grimly, but said no more, hurrying up the steep path in the same way he'd come.

Lauren watched him disappear over the top. She wasn't going to hold her breath waiting for his visit. When it came to business, she knew exactly where she stood—dead last.

# five

Lauren listened as hard rain pelted the galvanized roof of the cabin. The vengeful sound turned deafening at times, much like her own thoughts, loud and overwhelming. Lauren let the calico print curtain drop lazily back into place as she turned from the rain-blurred window. One wary glance at the clock let her know Jason's two hours had come and gone. Not that she really expected him to come on time.

Jason was perpetually late. Lauren was forever punctual. It was a subject they'd actively debated in years past and one she couldn't win. Of course, there was always a legitimate excuse for his lateness. How could she compete with success?

Five o'clock! If she were truly honest, there was a sense of relief mixed in with the anxiety she felt over the delay. The first two hours had given her time to better sort the complexity of the situation. In less than six hours Lauren had learned some cold truths—truths she never expected nor really wanted to believe.

Jason was a total mystery. He'd admitted knowing her whereabouts over the past years, going as far to say her address was blazed into his memory, yet he never bothered to phone or see her. It simply didn't make sense. Could he have been so put out by Lauren's supposed rejection of Tara's apology that he'd written her off completely? If only he'd called, himself.

But most intriguing was the house. Lauren hadn't missed the almost sad quality present in Jason's voice when she'd touched heavily on the subject. Yet he'd never given her an answer as to why. If he hadn't built it for spite, then for what? He certainly hadn't built the house for her. It was obvious he still held great contempt for her and had ill-judged her—again.

Another thought crossed Lauren's mind. Who was the black-haired beauty on the cliff? Had Lauren imagined the tension this woman created or how abruptly Jason tried to shoo her away? Something akin to jealousy sparked through her at the thought. Who was she and why was she at the house? Jason had all but given Lauren the bum's rush after the woman's arrival.

Lauren walked aimlessly back to the window, peering out with unseeing eyes. Why should she even care who the woman was? Jason and she weren't in love anymore. That fact was indisputable. She'd once heard it was impossible to fall out of love, just as it was to fall in love. Lauren supposed it to be true. But their love hadn't fallen from anywhere; it had been crushed into millions of tiny pieces before finally being ground into fine dust. There was nothing repairable about that!

Lauren had always believed God's will dictated there was one man for every woman, but her experience with Jason shot down that belief pretty quickly too. She'd loved Jason with all her heart and yet, over time, she'd found another to love, hadn't she? She'd been so sure at the time Jason was the one, the one she'd be spending the rest of her living days with. God's blessing had been upon them, she'd felt sure of it. But it never happened, and Lauren had learned her first real lesson about trusting reality, not emotions. How could her feelings have been so misguided? Wasn't true love supposed to conquer everything, even scandals and desperate misunderstandings?

The shrill ring of the phone cut through her thoughts. Lauren looked at the clock again. There was little doubt in her mind who the caller would be, excuse in hand—of course.

But it wasn't Jason's voice she heard on the line.

"I see you've made it safe and sound!" Tom greeted her happily. "Did you have a nice trip over to the island?"

Lauren strained to hear as the rain seemed to increase in strength, pounding the roof without mercy. "Tom, I'm so glad you called," she finally responded, plugging one ear with her finger. She pressed the receiver even tighter to the other ear. "And yes, the boat trip was fine."

"What's all that racket?" he asked loudly. "Sounds like a freight train coming through."

"A storm's blowing in across the lake, and it's pouring buckets right now." Lauren stretched the cord as far as it would go to the kitchen table. "How are things in Cincinnati?" A pang of homesickness nettled at her heart.

There was laughter in his reply. "Worried the college can't get along without their best accountant?" he asked. "Everything seemed well under control when I went by there this afternoon for my exam."

"Oh, Tom," she immediately interrupted. "How did your first orals go?" She grimaced guiltily. She'd forgotten about his exams, neglected to pray for him. It was inexcusable.

"Pretty well," he answered. "It's just one of those things where you answer all the questions to the best of your ability and hope you gave them what they were looking for. At least day one is down, and I only have two more to go." The noisy rain died down, and his voice grew softer. "I appreciated your prayers. I could really feel them today."

Lauren bit her lip in self-reproach. The prayers he felt weren't hers at all. She'd been too enraptured with her own problems to even remember. It was as if she'd stepped from one life into another, the latter as disjointed and lost as the first. "I'm sure you did very well, Tom," she finally said. "You always do."

"Such faith in your man. I like that." Tom laughed amiably.

Lauren was glad Tom couldn't see the worried expression on her face. An uneasy feeling tapped at her gut, a feeling of uncertainty. She disliked it when he spoke possessively like that. His words, although innocent, seemed to ensnare her. By rights, any woman would be thrilled with the prospect of being possessed by a man like Tom.

But she wasn't! And she feared their relationship was about to change. Would she be the same woman after a week on Bay Island?

Tom seemed to sense her troubled thoughts. "Have you talked with anyone on the island?"

"I met Tilly earlier," she answered hesitantly. "And I've seen Jason."

"Oh?" Lauren detected a bit of caution in his low voice. "How did it go?"

"Not very well, I'm afraid." Her fingers doodled imaginary circles on the maple kitchen table as she gave Tom a rough sketch of the events and information she'd learned that day. "As you can see, I'm not quite sure what to make of it. My name's already been cleared. Technically, my objective for coming here has been met." She paused thoughtfully. "Maybe I should come home."

There was an audible sigh. "No, you need to stay right where you are." His voice grew terribly serious and weighty. "It doesn't sound as if much of anything has been resolved. There's still more work to be done, a few more wrinkles to iron out." He paused. "Are you going to church tomorrow?"

Lauren let out a soft groan. "Yes, as much as I dread going." She could only picture the scene in her mind, how the church members would react. Would they greet her openly, offering their apologies, or would they ignore her, shying away in embarrassment? Either scenario made for an unpleasant morning.

"You can do it!" he encouraged. "I know it's been hard, but you'll be so much happier when this whole thing has been flushed out of your system." Tom's voice turned teasing. "Then we can get on with more important business, if you know what I mean. I was thinking a small grass-hut wedding in Africa or Bangladesh might be fun."

Lauren cringed. There he went again.

"I was only joking, Lauren," he quipped, obviously sensing

her silent discomfort. "You know I'd never push you into missions or marrying me. I'm a patient man, and I'm confident God will show us just what He wants before December."

"I'm sure He will," Lauren agreed. Relief tickled her heart. Five months seemed like a long reprieve at the moment.

A sudden, loud bang erupted from the front door. Lauren's startled gaze darted nervously toward the noise.

"Can you hold a minute, Tom?" She put the receiver on the table without waiting for his reply.

Lauren stopped dead in her tracks as the door jolted open without warning and a tall, blue-slickered figure barged purposefully inside. Blatant fear tore through her until she recognized Jason's face emerging from under the rain-soaked hood. Large drops of water cascaded off the slicker and onto the floor, instantly forming puddles at his feet. Jason held a drenched cardboard pizza box in one wet hand.

"Take this, would you, please," he instructed, shoving the box toward her.

Lauren took the drooping box as her racing heart and senses began recovery. "Let me get you a towel." Quickly she deposited the pizza on the kitchen counter and disappeared down the short hallway to the bathroom. She emerged a moment later with a large brown towel.

Jason shrugged the dripping slicker off his shoulders.

"Let me take that," Lauren said, exchanging the wet slicker for the dry towel. "You're drenched."

He gave a wry chuckle. "Tell me something I don't already know."

Lauren hurried through the kitchen and into the utility room with the raincoat. "I didn't know it was supposed to rain like this," she called loudly as she reached for the coat hook. Returning, Lauren gazed across the large room which served as the living, dining, and kitchen area. She watched Jason towel-dry his blond hair.

"They didn't predict this much rain," he responded, now

wiping the towel down his glistening arms. He glanced at the kitchen clock. "I tried waiting it out but finally gave it up. I didn't want to keep you waiting any longer." His comment held a double meaning which wasn't lost on her.

"You could have called," she told him. But then again, he was always good with excuses. There was no sense bringing it up. "It doesn't matter anyway. As long as you're here now."

Jason's gaze riveted to the kitchen table. "Did I interrupt something?"

Lauren let her eyes follow his line of vision. The phone! She'd forgotten Tom! Warmth crept up her neck. "I am on the phone. Just—just make yourself comfortable." She looked uncertainly at his wet clothes. "Dad still has a couple shirts and shorts in the back closet if you want those. They're probably a bit musty-smelling, but at least they're dry." She seriously doubted Jason would fit comfortably into her father's extra-large clothes.

"I'll be in the bathroom, changing," he announced, looking pointedly at the phone. "Don't keep him waiting."

Lauren cast Jason a quick, surprised look, but didn't respond. She was sure she'd heard a soft chuckle before he vanished down the hall and into the walk-in closet.

Lauren kept a wary eye toward the hallway as she returned to the phone. "I'm sorry, Tom," Lauren rushed, her voice low. "I didn't mean to keep you waiting."

"Was that Jason I heard?"

Another wave of warmth crept upward. "Yes. He just came in." She felt awkward and uncomfortable. "He's changing out of his—his wet clothes." She stopped for one horrified second. "I don't mean in here! In the bathroom, of course." Immediately she rolled her eyes. *What is wrong with me?*

"It's okay," Tom responded with a reassuring laugh. "I'm not the jealous type."

Nervously, Lauren tucked a strand of hair behind her ear. "There's certainly no reason for you to be jealous."

"You almost sound hurt that I'm not," he teased. "I suppose I could show a little jealousy if that'd make you feel any better. Might be good for your ego, you know. Is that what you want?" he asked, giving a full laugh.

Lauren imagined his grinning face, dark and handsome, the large dimple on his cheek deepening. "No."

"You forget, my dear Lauren, I trust you implicitly, no matter what or how the circumstances appear." The amusement had left his voice, and Lauren caught his meaning full force. Before she could respond, he went on. "I knew going into this you'd have to meet with Jason— probably more than once, but it's a gamble I'm willing to take." His lighter tone returned. "Just make sure he's out of there by midnight, Cinderella. I may not be the jealous type, but I do have my limits." Another easy laugh came across the line. "There! Is that enough jealousy to keep your ego intact?"

Lauren smiled to herself. "More than enough." Movement caught her eye, drawing her gaze toward the figure coming down the hallway.

Jason walked into the open room, stopping to give her a full, modeling twirl. The oversized clothes swirled loosely with him, sagging terribly on his tall frame. His eyebrows inched upward quizzically for an opinion. Lauren gave him a warning glance, but found it hard to keep the smile off her face.

"Lauren?" Tom's voice brought her back.

"Sorry."

"I'll call you Monday evening about the same time. Will you be around?"

"I'll be here," she answered distractedly.

Lauren watched as Jason traipsed into the kitchen and turned on the oven before rummaging loudly through the cookware cabinet. He finally produced a round pizza pan and quickly stripped the pizza from the soggy box and placed it on the pan before throwing it into the oven.

"I may have to visit the library Monday," Tom continued on, oblivious to her lack of attention. "If I do, it may be eight or later before I get home to make the call."

Jason walked silently to the back porch door, coming back a few seconds later, his arms full of kindling wood.

*What is he doing?* She wondered if he'd lost his mind.

"And, Lauren?"

"Hmm?" she answered absentmindedly.

Jason walked past her and deposited the kindling in the holder by the fireplace. His eyes danced mischievously, obviously fully aware of the distraction he was making.

"Remember to pray on Monday. I need to pass these orals."

Lauren snapped her attention back. "I'll be praying for you all day, I really will." Did Tom suspect she'd neglected him in prayer today? Struggling hard to keep her focus from Jason who was lighting the dry twigs in the fireplace, she turned her back on him. But her mind refused to budge. Why was Jason lighting the fireplace in July? For the first time, she noticed the cold draft invading the room, most surely brought on by the northern storm.

"Take good care of yourself," Tom instructed, interrupting her thoughts once again.

"I will," Lauren responded. Her voice softened out of Jason's hearing range. "I really miss you, Tom. Take care until I come back."

Tom murmured something in response and hung up. She was still clinging to the phone when Jason passed her again with another load of firewood. The wood dropped noisily into the basket as she slowly replaced the receiver.

"I'm warming the pizza," Jason commented when she walked into the room. "Thought a small fire might chase away the cold."

"That's fine, Jason," she responded casually, relieved at the evenness in her voice. "I see you found the clothes all right."

"Don't see how these kids today function with loose

britches," he said, adjusting the waistband as he hunkered down to tend the fire. "How do they keep these things on?"

Lauren only shrugged, wondering if Jason's bantering was for his benefit or hers. She'd do well to remember he still had a lot of explaining to do.

At Lauren's ambiguous shrug, Jason stood abruptly from his squatting position. "I suppose you're ready to get on with it," he taunted gently.

"Yes," she answered bluntly.

A grim expression overtook his face. "Well, I'm not!"

Lauren gave him a sharp glance. "What do you mean?"

"Not on an empty stomach, I'm not." Jason breezed past her to the kitchen, leaving a bemused Lauren behind. "I think better on a full stomach."

# six

"Have you got any pop?" Jason rummaged through the kitchen drawers, finally pulling out paper plates and napkins.

*Just make yourself at home, why don't you?* Lauren was tempted to say it aloud as she stared silently at the man's back. Since Jason's arrival, he'd buzzed about the cabin as if their five-year separation had never occurred. Something was wrong with this carefree, amicable behavior. Just that afternoon he'd been unflinchingly cool, and now he was forcing levity into the atmosphere.

Lauren walked carefully past him, maintaining a fair distance. "I'm sure there's some pop in the fridge, but it's probably not the kind you like." She opened the refrigerator door, staring at the contents. A frown crept over her lips. Figures! She pulled out a can of her favorite and one of his. "Guess you're in luck."

A satisfied grin spread over his face. "Doesn't sound like you were the one doing the shopping. It must have been my guardian angel who was so thoughtful."

"No, it was Tilly," she responded with some exasperation. Tilly's initiative to also buy some of Jason's brand of soda, one she herself detested, bothered her greatly. There had to be an unhealthy, preconceived idea somewhere in Tilly's mind about her and Jason. It could only mean trouble.

His mouth quirked. "Sometimes angels come in different forms."

Lauren ignored his attempt at humor by searching through the hutch for a trivet. A moment later she heard the oven door creak open.

"I don't know about you," he called out to her, "but I don't plan to stand around in the kitchen exchanging pleasantries all day. I'm hungry and I mean to eat."

47

She placed a large silver trivet in the middle of the dining room table and glanced into the kitchen. "The pot holder's in the middle. . ." The words died away as she caught his intent stare.

"I know," he assured, his words a mere whisper.

*Of course he knows,* she thought with a sigh. He knew every nook and cranny of the kitchen, maybe even better than she did.

Jason slowly opened the middle drawer and pulled out a flowery pot holder. Lauren watched him drag the hot pizza pan from the oven and move quickly from the kitchen, right past her and the table, and into the living area. Hot steam trailed behind him.

"Where are you going?"

"In front of the fireplace. Where else?"

Lauren stepped back, her voice taunting. "Just like old times?"

Jason gave a slight start as he lowered the pizza onto the stone ledge of the fireplace. He turned slowly, his dark gaze penetrating. There was an awful silence. "No," he finally said. "We both know the good old days can't be brought back again. But if you'll remember, we did call for a temporary truce. I thought it'd be nice to sit by the fireplace. If you object—"

"No," Lauren said contritely. "It's all right." Without hesitation, Lauren brought over the two sodas and plopped herself down on the carpeted edge of the flagstone. Why did she have the feeling Jason was gaining the upper hand on the evening?

Jason fed the fire once more before securing the fire screen. "Still take your pizza with pepperoni, peppers, and double cheese?" he asked, scooping several small squares. He handed her the plate.

Lauren looked thoughtfully at the pizza he gave her. "You still remember?"

She felt the odd look Jason gave her, but he said nothing as he filled his own plate. Slowly he lowered himself to the floor. "Of course, I remember," he finally answered. "It's a little early in the ball game to have my memory going." The corner of his mouth lifted slightly. "We consumed more than our share of pizzas in the past. It would be hard to forget." There was something playful and tender in his tone.

Lauren's heart tugged at its warmth. "We did eat our fair share." She picked up a piece and examined it. "I've added Italian sausage to my repertoire. Didn't want anyone to think I was in a rut."

"I'll keep the new information on file." He watched as she took a bite.

Lauren held his gaze for a long second before finally breaking eye contact. She looked down at her plate again in silence. Not a companionable silence, but a stiff, prelude silence that waited for the inevitable. She couldn't help but wonder what he was thinking. Meeting him like this was harder than she'd imagined, and her emotional energies were ebbing fast—just when her defenses needed to be at their greatest.

"You're not eating." Jason's glance lighted on her.

"To be honest, Jason," Lauren admitted, setting the paper plate down, "my stomach's been in knots ever since this trip was planned."

"Then why did you come?" he asked much too casually.

Lauren had no intention of explaining Tom's request. She'd already said too much. She couldn't very well admit her fears to Jason. By all rights, he was still her adversary. She was right to be wary of him. Jason had been in a position to search out the truth five years ago, but instead, he'd cast her aside, treating her as a pathetic liar who was totally expendable. He deserved her animosity. Why, then, did loneliness rush in on her as she looked at Jason's waiting expression?

"You wouldn't understand," she finally said with resignation.

"Try me!"

Lauren sighed. How could she sum up the honest reasons as to why she'd come back? True, Tom had firmly nudged her into action, but if the truth were to be told, she'd come to face the ghosts of her former life. If she faced them, maybe, just maybe she could finally shut the door to their existence.

"What's happening in your life now?" Jason prodded again. "Something's made this trip necessary."

"Maybe."

Jason opened the fire screen and stirred the fire with the poker. "It only makes sense, Lauren. Five years is a long time to break total contact with the island and then," he paused, snapping his fingers for emphasis, "all of a sudden show up. Something's occurred in your well-ordered life to spur you into action."

"My well-ordered life?" she repeated blankly.

"Your life has always been ordered," Jason told her pointedly. "You like all your ducks in a neat, little row."

Lauren had to stop this maddening line of conversation. He was creating a diversion from her true mission, delaying the explanations due on his side.

"Although I'm sure my orderly life is of great interest," she began with a bit of sarcasm, "it's the issue of false accusations that brings me here." Lauren let her fingers glide nervously over the flagstone. "But in a sense you're right. I am at a point in my life where I'd like to move on without Bay Island hanging around my neck like an anchor."

"So you've come to set the record straight?"

"In a nutshell—yes."

"And you say you've never heard anything from anyone on Bay Island in five years?" Jason sat relaxed—too relaxed—his long legs stretched out lazily, crossed at the ankles. "Could it be that a special someone in your life has spurred you on after all these years?"

Lauren didn't like the way Jason was interrogating her once more. If there were to be any more cross-examinations, she'd be the one doing the questioning—not Jason. "I haven't come to discuss my life with you, Jason, but to find out why things happened as they did five years ago. I had no knowledge of Tara's death or her confession to you and the church."

But Jason was persistent. "You didn't receive a call from Tara?"

"I told you, Jason," she responded, exasperated, "Tara never called me. I never spoke to her."

He looked perplexed for a moment. "I don't understand it."

"Has the possibility ever crossed your mind, Tara may not have made the call?" Lauren pointed out logically. "We've both seen, firsthand, Tara's talents in the area of deception. Could it be possible she was still protecting what was dear to her?" Her voice dwindled to a soft sigh. "She was in love with you. You'll admit that now, won't you?"

Jason looked at her coolly. "Let's not go into that again."

"How can we avoid it?" Lauren sat up straight and leaned forward. "I was a threat to her, Jason, and as much as I tried to tell you, you couldn't see it. The whole scheme she'd pulled off was for one purpose, and one purpose only—to get rid of me. Without me, you were free again. Maybe she was still holding on to that. Maybe she feared I'd come running back to you once this mess was finally cleared."

"Ready to start all over again, is that it?" he finished for her, disbelief on his tone.

"Something like that."

There was a moment of silence as his gaze seem to pierce her very being. "Would you have come back?"

Lauren let her gaze drop pensively toward the bright flames of fire before shaking her head. "Five years is a long time," she whispered, her voice husky. "My life's changed—I've changed. You've changed." She slowly turned toward him. "And you hurt me, Jason, like no man ever has or ever will again. A hurt like that doesn't just go away—not even with time." Lauren stopped, aghast at what she'd just admitted.

Jason sat up from his relaxed position, letting his hands dangle thoughtfully between his knees. "I'll never be able to live down what I allowed to happen to you," he freely conceded, his face grim. "I may not be able to assume all the fault, Tara had her share, but it ultimately fell to me to determine how to handle the situation. I managed it badly. I protected my pride more than anything else." He raked his long fingers thoughtfully through his hair. "I can't tell you how many times I've asked God for His forgiveness."

Lauren glanced up sharply, leveling him with an accusing look. "And what about my forgiveness? Did you ever think to ask for my forgiveness?" There was an aching pause. "Why didn't you call me, Jason? Why didn't you tell me you were sorry?"

Jason slowly rubbed one hand over his bristly chin, the five-o'clock shadow making the defined angles that much more prominent. "I'd planned to."

"When?" Lauren scoffed. "Next week? Next year?"

"After Tara talked with you," he answered, his voice dropping a decibel lower, "I'd planned to call you."

"And?"

"And then Tara phoned you."

Her gaze swept over him. "You wrote me off after she'd told you of my horrible behavior. Is that it?" Lauren couldn't believe it. How could Jason be taken in not once, but twice? "You never questioned the validity of her story?"

Jason frowned at her. "You weren't there, Lauren. Tara did change after coming to Jesus." With a defeated sigh, he rubbed his chin again. "Would you have me believe she faked it all, and in the end, died without Christ?" It was clear the possibility not only appalled but frightened him. He shook his head. "I won't believe that."

"You'd rather believe Tara than me?"

"I didn't say that." He looked at her crossly, his tone turning icy. "You keep making it sound like a contest exists between you two. Lauren, the woman's dead."

*And she's still wreaking havoc in my life!* Jason could be so dense at times. "I didn't say that," Lauren retorted, taking the chance to steal his own line. "But maybe you're right. How can I compete for the truth when you never give my reasoning a chance? Why is it so hard for you to believe me?"

When he spoke, his tone thawed, but the taunting inflection remained. "I do believe you about the phone call, Lauren." He released an exaggerated sigh. "I don't understand it, and I'm not ready to brand Tara a fake, but I do believe you."

Lauren detected the catch in his voice. It gave her a small stab of satisfaction to know she'd rattled his cool exterior. "Thank you for saying so."

He looked at her thoughtfully. "What would you have said to Tara if you'd gotten the call?"

"I'm not sure," she answered honestly. "I'd like to say I would have forgiven her, given her a proper Christian response, but that little self-righteous pat on the back would be just that." Right now she didn't feel very Christ-like toward Tara, and she wondered if she'd ever allow God to help her in that area. As draining as the emotion of hate was, it seemed easier to handle and maintain than the alternative. Forgiving Tara would require more than she possessed. Wasn't she entitled to keep what little pride she had left?

"You couldn't, or should I say, wouldn't, have forgiven her?" The question seemed to be of great importance to him.

"I was never given the chance to find out what I would have done," she answered evasively.

Jason appeared to reflect upon her words. The crackling of the fire seemed to grow more intense in the silence. "I was with her when she died, you know."

Lauren said nothing but kept her eyes fixed on the fire. She hoped Jason wasn't going into any gruesome details meant to rip at her heartstrings.

"I think I was angrier with you as she lay dying than I was when I'd thought you'd sold my drawings." Sadness vibrated in his voice.

"Me!" Lauren gave a low cry, her tired heart reeling.

"She wasn't at peace, Lauren," Jason continued on. "She couldn't accept God's forgiveness without yours. I tried to tell her she'd done her best, that God would deal with the rest. She just couldn't see past it."

"Yet you never called me!" she stated incredulously.

"No," he answered, seeming to struggle for the right words. "That was the day I finally let you go. What little spark of hope, existed died right there in that hospice room."

There was an awkward silence.

"And where are we supposed to go from here?" Lauren whispered.

"Forward, I hope," he answered pragmatically.

"I don't think it could go backward any further," she reasoned in all seriousness.

As if against his will, he smiled. "Don't tempt it."

Lauren gave him a nervous smile. Things could be worse. Or could they? "Do the people at church know about this phone call business with Tara?"

"No," he answered without hesitancy. "They just assumed things went all right, that everything was patched up between Tara and you. I'm sure some began to wonder, though, when you never came back."

"Well, I'm here now." She sighed wearily. "But little good it does at this point. The past can't be fixed."

"No, but we can alter the future." Jason stood, picking up the cold pizza pan. "Tomorrow I'm picking you up for church. That's the first obstacle to be dealt with. Secondly, I plan to find out what happened to the call you were supposed to receive from Tara."

Lauren stood and followed Jason into the kitchen. "How do you plan to do that?"

Jason ripped off a long sheet of aluminum foil. "I'm not sure yet, but I'll figure out something." Quickly he wrapped the uneaten portions. "And thirdly, I plan to enjoy the Skipper's Festival this week, regardless. I'll show you just how much I've improved my rock-skipping skills."

Lauren smiled. "You're still competing?"

"Yes. And I plan to win this year." He opened the refrigerator door.

"Jason?"

"Hmm?"

Lauren watched as he slid the leftovers on the top shelf before looking up expectantly. "Why did you build our—your house?"

His expression sobered. "That I don't plan to explain right now. I think we've got enough on our plates, so to speak, to deal with."

Lauren nodded silently, wondering, yet refusing to ask about the woman she'd seen at his home. Jason disappeared into the utility room, then reappeared with his blue slicker.

"Services start at ten," Jason said, opening the front door. "I'll be by at nine-thirty."

Lauren followed him out onto the wooden deck, their steps echoing softly in the darkness. "The rain seems to have stopped."

Jason nodded and took a deep breath as he looked up at the sky. "There's something so pure about the air after a good rain," he said softly. He leaned on the rail and looked out. "I've missed the view from Piney Point." Slowly he turned toward her, his dark eyes deepening. "And I've really missed you, Lauren." She held her breath. "I'm glad you've come back."

An emotional lump was closing in on Lauren's tight throat. *Oh, please don't let me cry.* The threat subsided for a moment allowing her to speak with a steady, clear voice. "I've missed you too."

Jason moved closer. He reached out and rested his warm hands gently on her arms. "And I am truly sorry for the way I treated you and how this whole ugly mess turned out." He pulled her an inch closer. "Will you ever be able to forgive me?"

"I told you five years ago I'd already forgiven you," she replied in a near whisper. *Just please don't ask me to forgive Tara.*

He searched over her face, his expression unreadable. "I don't believe you really have, and I'm not letting you leave this time until you do. I plan to make this up to you, Lauren."

"That won't be necess—"

"Yes, it is necessary," he said with conviction. Soft night sounds surrounded them, echoing as he slowly lowered his face to hers.

Lauren knew what was coming. Paralyzed, she let his lips brush lightly across hers, neither refusing nor responding.

"I will make this up to you, Lauren Wright. I promise!" With that, he bounded off the deck, down the wet steps, and to his car. "Nine-thirty! Be ready."

Lauren watched the road for several minutes after the sedan's taillights vanished into the darkness. Fear gripped at her heart. Jason's presence, his touch, his kiss—what was she to do? Her mind refused to believe, but her heart knew the awful truth. She was still in love with Jason Levitte!

# seven

"You look nice," Jason commented, swinging open the passenger door. "Blue has always been a good color for you."

Lauren murmured a polite response as she eased herself into the passenger seat. Instantly she felt the cool texture of the leather upholstery as it penetrated her lightweight skirt. The fresh morning air still held a damp chill.

Stress and fatigue—due to her maddeningly sleepless night—were taking their toll on Lauren's resolve. Thoughts of Tara had roved through her mind all night like a wolf on the prowl. Would it ever be possible to know the truth about the mysterious phone call? Was there any way to prove her own innocence? The taunting thoughts would not settle. It was like being accused all over again.

Jason had been with Tara when the call had supposedly been made. Lauren racked her brain for possible scenarios. The only person who could have possibly intercepted such a call would have been her sister, Cassie. But she'd only lived with Lauren for a brief, two-month period. A possible but not probable conclusion. And Cassie would have told Lauren if such a call had come. There was no explanation. Was Tara lying? Could she have fooled Jason with a dial tone pressed to her ear?

Jason slipped into the car, disrupting her thoughts. He paused to look at her. "Ready?"

"I suppose." Lauren rested her elbow on the door and rubbed her fingers along her temple. The headache plaguing her earlier seemed to step up a beat. An unnerving morning lay ahead, the next dreaded step she knew she must take.

"They're just sinners saved by grace," Jason said with a reassuring smile, seeming to perceive her thoughts. "Just like us." He grasped her hand and gave it a squeeze. "If it's any comfort, this is as hard for them as it is for you. They were really embarrassed and ashamed about how they treated you. Give them a chance to make it right."

Lauren was very aware of Jason's touch, his hand still firmly clutching hers. "I've tried hard to prepare myself for this, but I'm not looking forward to it." She took a deep breath, paused, and took three curious, successive sniffs. "Why does your car smell like fried chicken?"

"Probably because there's a pan of fried chicken in the trunk." He flashed her a knowing smile. "I've become a cook of sorts over the past few years."

Lauren waited for a further explanation, but it never came. "Maybe I'm better off not knowing," she mumbled softly to herself.

Jason released her hand, still smiling. Quickly he started the engine and maneuvered the sedan easily down the incline. "I don't always carry chicken around in my car," he baited.

"Oh?"

"Only for special events." He gave her a sidelong glance. "It's for the fellowship dinner after the morning service."

Lauren quickly turned toward him. "You never mentioned anything about a fellowship dinner," she groaned. Her temples began to throb harder. It was one thing to get through an hour-long service, and another to manage a fellowship meal.

He turned the car down Shore Lane. "You have to give the people a little time to get their nerve up, Lauren." His tone turned tender. "You'll do just fine—trust me. The fellowship time will give them an opportunity to talk with you, to be more relaxed. Then, by next Sunday, things will be much smoother." He laughed. "It may take Mr. Edwards at least that long to get his apology out."

Mr. Edwards! Lauren closed her eyes to block out the old man's image. The church elder had actually stood in front of the entire congregation and demanded her removal from the church roster.

It was utterly devastating. The man had shown her no mercy.

"If Mr. Edwards needs more time, he'll be too late," Lauren said flatly, leaning back against the headrest. "I won't be here next week."

Jason snapped his head toward her. "What do you mean?"

"I'm only here for a week," Lauren explained matter-of-factly. "I thought you knew."

"A week!" he sputtered incredulously, frowning. "How did you ever figure to straighten out this mess in a week?"

Lauren gave him a level, logical look. "I didn't figure on anything." She could tell he was disturbed by her nonchalance. "I know a week isn't long—"

"Of course, a week isn't long enough," he interrupted. He rapped his long fingers impatiently on the steering wheel. "We have a lot to work through." He paused and looked at her. "And what about the Skipper's Festival? You said you'd come."

"Oh, I'll be here for the festival." It was the old Jason talking now—concerned and commanding. And she had to admit, he looked unbearably handsome in his blue pin-striped suit. Combined with the thick halo of blond waves, the attraction was nearly too much. Lauren raised her eyebrows playfully. "I wouldn't miss your performance for anything. You might actually win the title this year."

Jason didn't smile, but focused his smoky gray eyes on the road ahead. "Is there something—or someone—causing you to rush back so soon?"

Lauren knew the question was loaded. She certainly missed Tom, but not enough to rush home. And right now she didn't want to talk about Tom. The memory of Jason's kiss the night before was still too vivid to spoil—just yet.

"I'm on a week's vacation," she finally said. "There's a job to consider. I can't just take off when I want."

Jason wore an expression that told her he knew better. "A week just isn't going to be long enough." He seemed to pause and mull over the situation. "I'll take some time off this week. I don't want you leaving before I've had time to make things up to you."

Lauren smiled, inexplicably pleased. Then the smile slipped. How many times in the past had Jason expressed his wish to spend time with her, only to have his work suddenly intrude? And there was another woman to consider. Surely the woman wouldn't sit idly by as he divided his attention between the two. How did he plan to handle that?

Jason waited.

"I told you before. There's no need to make anything up," Lauren said slowly. "I know how important your work is to you." She looked distractedly out her window. The morning was alive with colorful summer flowers, all but unseen in her preoccupation.

"I'm not married to it," Jason responded, sounding a trifle annoyed. "The business is on its feet. It doesn't need the constant pampering it used to."

Lauren wasn't convinced. Just yesterday they'd been interrupted with company business, and they hadn't even been together for more than fifteen minutes. Still, if he could pull it off. . . The possibility of spending the week with Jason sent warmth through her veins. "You're liable to get a lot tongues wagging if people see us together." A forced smile hid the weightiness of her next words. "Besides, you might have a special someone who wouldn't like it very much."

"Not exactly subtle, are you?" he deadpanned.

Lauren couldn't tell from his tone whether he was irritated or amused. "About as subtle as you, I believe."

There was a brief silence before Jason slowly shook his head. "Don't worry yourself. I can handle things on my end. It's rather complicated and much too hard to explain." He glanced at her. "And what about you? Is your special someone okay with this trip?"

"My special someone," she began hesitantly, "trusts me explicitly."

A pained expression crossed his face, and she immediately

wished the words hadn't spilled out as they had. She hadn't meant to say it in such a way to hurt Jason. An appropriate retraction was forming when he interrupted.

"It's certainly a good thing he didn't see us kissing last night, then." Jason kept his eyes on the road, but Lauren could see their impish twinkle. He was actually enjoying her discomfort.

"Or her, either," Lauren retorted.

Jason faked a sigh of relief. "Or her, either!"

The atmosphere suddenly lightened, and they both smiled.

"Tell you what," Jason suggested. "Our own problems are complicated enough. Why don't we abandon the rest of our outside dilemmas for this week? It will be just you and me."

As he spoke, Lauren watched the church whiz by. She stretched her neck and thumbed back toward it. "You just passed the church."

Jason hit the brakes and looked in the rearview mirror. "See what you've done?" A slow grin crept over his face as he quickly wheeled the car back around. "Well? What do you say to my proposal?"

"Just you and me, huh?" Lauren met his teasing eyes with a smile. She liked the idea immensely. She knew it was emotional suicide at best, but how could her heart refuse? She wanted to be with Jason. Ramifications could be dealt with later. She stuck her hand out before him. "Deal!"

Jason looked quickly from her face to outstretched hand, a smile playing across his lips. He gave her hand a firm shake. "Deal!"

Lauren watched as the church whizzed by once more. "You just passed the church—again," she announced.

Their gazes locked and both broke out in laugher.

❧

The church building was packed as Lauren scanned the crowd, seeing several new faces mixed with the old. Jason held his hand reassuringly on the small of her back as he guided her through the foyer. An unfamiliar woman took their food dish, and they proceeded into the sanctuary. For a moment their presence went unnoticed until Larry Newkirk intercepted them.

"It's good to see you again," Larry greeted, his warm smile aimed at Lauren. His gaze traced the length of Jason's arm, lingering at her waist. He nodded. "Jason."

Was it her imagination, or was there tension between the two men? Lauren shot a nervous glance at Jason. Jason, however, seemed perfectly at ease.

"How's the police job, Larry?" Jason asked in a light and friendly tone.

"Same as usual," Larry briefly responded before turning back to Lauren. "I forgot to mention yesterday when I saw you that I have something of yours you'll want back."

Puzzled, Lauren slowly shook her head. "Something of mine?"

"Your cross necklace," Larry explained. "You'd lost it during a drama rehearsal one night. Remember?"

Remember! Of course she remembered. It had been a graduation gift from her parents, which she'd worn daily for several years. Hopelessly she'd searched the church for weeks. When she'd left the island, she'd given it up for lost, as lost as her faith.

"That's wonderful, Larry," she gushed with anticipation. "Do you have it with you?"

"Sorry," he apologized. "I didn't think to bring it." He looked meaningfully at Jason before turning back to her. "I can swing by the cabin sometime this week with it if that'd be okay."

"Sure," Lauren answered hesitantly, feeling the increased pressure from Jason's hand on her back. "I'm here for the week." She glanced at Jason. He stood perfectly poised.

"I'll be sure to catch you before then."

They only exchanged pleasantries for a moment more before Larry wandered off to a beckoning friend and Jason ushered her further down the aisle toward the front.

"Better be careful with Larry," he whispered close to her ear. Lauren drew her brows together in bewilderment.

He moved closer. "He's always had a thing for you."

"A thing?" It took everything within her to keep a skeptical chortle from erupting. "Jason, he was a drama student of mine, just a kid." Of all the ridiculous. . .

Jason kept propelling them down the aisle. "He's not a kid now!"

Lauren could feel several pairs of eyes trained on her back, and she said no more. Right now she had other, weightier things to deal with. She found her stomach muscles forming into knots. What was she doing here? The once familiar building seemed foreign, distanced by more than time. The people were strangers, pieces of a past life she no longer knew.

"Is this okay?" Jason asked, stopping at the third pew from the front. Before she could protest, he whispered. "Go ahead and sit down. I'll be right back."

Pride kept Lauren from detaining him, and he hadn't waited for a reply before disappearing. A tremor of distress flitted through her. Was she losing her mind? In less than twenty-four hours she'd done an about-face with Jason. She was once again the unassuming, starry-eyed woman she used to be.

"Looks like you've patched things up with Jason."

Lauren looked up and was barely able to move out of the way before Tilly plopped herself down in the pew beside her.

Tilly gave her a wide smile. "It's good to be back, isn't it, Girl?"

Lauren nodded absently knowing Tilly wasn't paying one bit of attention to her response. Instead, Tilly was looking over the congregation. Much to Lauren's horror, Tilly silently began summoning several from their seats. It wasn't long before numerous faces swam before her, greeting, talking, laughing—causing absolute chaos in Lauren's mind. Each seemed caught up in Tilly's exuberance.

"Oh, we're so glad you're back," Mrs. Phillips, the church librarian, cooed. "We were just asking about you last week, weren't we Gertrude?" The older lady looked assuredly to the tall woman beside her who bobbed her head in agreement.

Lauren smiled. Both women had always reminded her of the two aunts in *Arsenic and Old Lace,* sweet and unassuming. "How have you both been?"

Neither got far into the conversation before the choir began filling the loft, dispersing the crowd.

Tilly squeezed Lauren's shoulder. "Told you everyone would welcome you back," she pronounced, slipping quickly out of the pew.

Lauren hazarded a look at her retreating back. Beyond, she caught a glimpse of the raven-haired woman in the back. Jason was at her side. Her heart sank. Lauren slowly faced forward. Once again, an immense wave of regret washed over her. She should have never come back. Up and down, back and forth. Soon she wouldn't know which way was anywhere.

The song leader was announcing the first hymn as Jason slipped quietly into the pew. Lauren kept her eyes fixed to the front. Still she couldn't hide the sight of him from her periphery. His presence, his control overwhelmed her. She felt him tap her arm.

"Sorry, I got tied up," he whispered when she turned toward him, his face a mock look of chagrin. He pulled out a blue hymnbook from its holder and held it before her.

Lauren wouldn't—couldn't—sing. The lump in her throat seemed to be growing by the second.

"Are you all right?" Jason was leaning close to her ear.

Lauren could feel his warm breath, smell the minty tang of a lozenge. She nodded, giving him a reassuring smile. He seemed convinced.

The service dragged, and Lauren forced herself not to look at her watch constantly. Her mind was too much in turmoil. Finally the closing prayer ended. But there was no escape.

Immediately, smiling faces accosted her as Jason kept the cordial introductions and updates coming. Lauren tried desperately to keep up each conversation but was hopelessly lost. No longer could Lauren discern the past actions of these people.

With the exception of Mr. Edwards, most of the accusations were behind her back or silent in nature. Were these the same people who had shunned her so mercilessly five years ago?

"I'm starving," Jason finally announced to the group. "There's plenty of time to talk with Lauren over lunch."

The group disbanded happily, and Jason turned to her. "They may not come right out and apologize, but they're mending fences just the same by their welcome. You can see that, can't you?"

"It's hard to tell between mending fences and sweeping it under the carpet," she replied honestly.

Was accepting her back into the church circle, into their fold again, enough to exonerate the past? She didn't think so. But Jason's question had been a rhetorical one. Regardless, she was now a stranger. Like leaving the parental home to be on your own, things are never the same again upon return. Relationships change. Unwritten rules change.

Jason quickly threaded them through the food line, making sure Lauren tried his fried chicken. Everyone seemed carefree and happy, as if the clouds had parted leaving sunshine in its place. Somehow, she managed through the fellowship dinner. It seemed more of a performance on her part. Even Mr. Edwards received a polite and appropriate response from her repertoire. She wanted to forgive these people—and some she could. But for others, their hurtful words and actions of the past paraded across Lauren's memory as they spoke with her. Her mouth managed the right responses, only they never quite reached her heart. *Oh, God, what if I can never forgive? Am I destined to be out of Your will forever?*

"It time to go." Jason was gently nudging her elbow. Lauren tried unsuccessfully to hide her damp eyes. He gave her a crooked grin, laying his arm lazily around her shoulders. "It feels good to get everything settled, doesn't it?"

Lauren gave a lying nod.

"Now," he said teasingly. "I believe our week is just starting. Let's not waste one minute of it."

# eight

True to his word, Jason became an attentive fixture at Piney Point the next day. The squeaky screen door, the loose deck boards, the leaky faucet—each yielded to his skillful hands. For Lauren it was just plain déjà vu.

"What's next?" Jason asked, backing himself out from under the sink cabinet. He looked expectantly at Lauren while wiping a rag over the plumbing wrench. He tossed the wrench noisily into the toolbox.

Lauren flipped three grilled cheese sandwiches on the griddle. "I think you've just about fixed everything there is to fix," she told him with a smile. "Get washed up for lunch. The sandwiches are almost done."

"Yes, Ma'am." He gave a mock salute and trotted off toward the bathroom.

Never in her wildest imagination had Lauren expected such a turnabout in Jason. Her heart was even more unprepared. She dreaded the fluttery feeling it gave every time he was near—a sure sign of impending disaster. And she was falling for his act. Where was her pride? Where was her sensibility? Jason was doing his best to make her stay on the island pleasant, but they couldn't just pick up where they left off. Yet what was she to do with the erupting feelings that mirrored her reawakening love—a love she thought had died? And what about Tom? The whole thing was getting much too complicated—just as she'd feared.

Jason reappeared in the kitchen as Lauren placed the coleslaw on the tray.

Jason picked up the tray. "I'll take that," he said with a charming smile. "Don't forget the napkins."

Lauren grabbed several paper napkins and followed him out to the front deck. The noon sun broke through the trees as swaying bits of puzzle-piece light danced over the picnic table. Jason set the tray down on the checkered tablecloth.

There was silence for several moments as they arranged the food. A warm, southerly breeze fluttered the paper plates until each one was properly laden with food.

Lauren looked up, venturing to speak first. "I saw Levitte's Landing when I came in on Saturday," she began. "It's really beautiful with all the walkways and dockside shops. When did you build it?"

"Finished it early last year," Jason answered, looking pleased at her interest. "I'm planning to expand the pier with two more restaurants and a couple of shops if the tourist numbers explode like last season." His enthusiasm seemed to ebb slightly, and he gave a careless shrug of his shoulder. "We'll see. I have a few other projects I might like to do first—maybe take some time off."

She nodded her understanding, noticing the change in his demeanor. Absent was the normal fervor he usually exhibited for his pet projects. Had Jason finally achieved a reasonable balance between work and his personal life or was something troubling him?

"I'd like to take you over there this afternoon," he continued on, a teasing glint in his eye. "I seem to remember how well you like shopping, and there are plenty of specialty stores to suit your fancy."

Lauren smiled. "I'd like that. I want to see the final design— all the details, you know. You certainly went through enough designing and redesigning. It should be perfect." She couldn't help but remember the many nights he'd worked and shared the drawings with her—cherishing each one as he would his own child. "I'm sure the final product's everything you wanted."

Jason raised an eyebrow but said nothing. His attention went back to his food.

Lauren shot him a nervous glance after a moment of silence settled in. "Are you ready to tell me about the house?" The house at Muriel's Inlet never left her mind. She'd looked for any opportunity to bring the subject up this morning, but Jason always seemed to head her off at the pass.

"No!" He took a sip of his drink, watching her over the rim of the glass.

She frowned as her gaze locked with his. Would he ever tell her? Jason shook his head at her as if to say he understood her questioning look. Lauren just stared back, contemplating her next move.

"Do you want to tell me about the woman—"

"No!"

Frustrated, Lauren leveled him with another stare. It was then she saw the spark of amusement crossing his face. The man was impossible.

"Is there anything we can talk about?" she asked with a smirk.

"No!" He smiled mischievously, and Lauren waited as he toyed mockingly with his coleslaw. "I take that back. We could talk about Cincinnati and the man—"

"No!" She jabbed her fork playfully in his direction.

"All right, then," he answered good-naturedly. "What's left?"

Lauren put her fork down and thought for a moment. Her mood suddenly grew serious. "Tell me about Tara. Tell me what happened."

Jason's brows creased over his half-hooded eyes, his reserve evident. "It will only start an argument, Lauren. I'm not sure we'll ever be able to agree to disagree. I do want to tell you about it—sometime. Now just doesn't seem like the right time."

"There will never be a right time," Lauren admitted with a sigh. "There are so many things I don't understand about what happened or about you, either. I need to know why."

Jason gave an elaborate sigh. Several emotions seemed to cross his tanned face as he sat contemplating.

"You're the one who said you wanted to make things up to me," she reminded gently. An insect buzzed her ear, and she absently shooed it away. "We have to start somewhere."

She sensed resignation in his voice when he finally spoke. "What do you want to know?"

"Everything," Lauren pleaded softly. "Tell me everything that happened after I left the island. Tell me about the people at the church. . .about Tara's illness." She poked her index finger at her chest. "Help me to understand."

Jason nodded. "I'm not sure anything I have to say will make you understand."

"Try me!" Lauren desperately wanted to clear the cloud between them, impossible as it seemed.

Jason shoved his food aside with a deep sigh. Silence reigned for several seconds. "The day you left was especially hard," he began reflectively. "But I really thought your leaving would be the end of it, a time to forget, a time to go on with my life. The church seemed to settle down from the scandal, the work remained steady, Tara stayed on as my secretary, and I hired a new accountant."

Lauren leaned forward, concentrating on his every word.

Jason swung one leg lazily over the bench before continuing on. "It was almost as if everything went back to normal until the day Tara was diagnosed with brain cancer. We didn't know at first it was cancer, but we knew it was serious. She said she smelled weird odors, and then the headaches came. The doctor ordered several tests and then a biopsy. By then it was too late."

"When did this all happen?" Lauren asked. The time frame was so important!

Jason squinted one eye in thought. "Almost three years after you left, I think. It all meshes together after awhile."

Lauren nodded. "Go on."

"Radiation shrank the tumor a little, and they tried to operate, but it was hopeless." He shook his head. "It was only a matter of time at that point. They gave her six months, maybe seven." He seemed to have difficulty forming his next thoughts. "Late one night after Tara realized death was inevitable, she called. She was so upset I couldn't make heads or tails of what she was saying. By the time I got there, she was hysterical. That's when the whole thing spilled out—how she hated you, what she'd done—how she'd set up the whole masterpiece."

Lauren picked up her glass of iced tea and took a sip. There were so many questions just begging to be asked. But she didn't dare interrupt.

"I don't think I need to go into detail about that." He took a sip of his own drink.

"Yes, you do," Lauren quickly corrected. "Tell me what she said."

Jason's jaw muscles tightened, and Lauren thought for a moment he wouldn't. Then something flickered in his eyes, and he began again. "I think you've already figured out how Tara borrowed your checkbook and rigged your account with the twenty thousand before setting up the last delivery. The rest wasn't too hard, and she'd kept herself pretty busy planting doubt in the minds of the other office staff as well. It was an elaborate scheme." There was an element of disbelief in his voice. "It's still so hard to fathom!"

"Did Tara ever tell you why?" Lauren asked softly.

He shook his head. "Not really. She mentioned something vague about trying to protect my interests, interests she thought you were somehow endangering." He shrugged one shoulder. "It really didn't make sense."

Lauren had to restrain the impulse to cry out. Instead she bit the inside of her lip purposely to slow her response. "She gave no details of her reasoning at all?" *There had to be signs, Jason!* "How did she act toward you after I left?" she prodded.

A brief look of annoyance crossed his face. "Lauren," he warned. "Let's not go there."

"Well," she encouraged cautiously, "just think for a moment." She met his brooding gaze. It was obvious Jason would have to be led by the hand on this one. "Did Tara stand by your side, pledging her loyal support after I left? Did she offer you solace at every turn? Was she magically at your side during every difficult moment?"

Jason looked at her and a laugh erupted. "Oh, come on, Lauren. You make it sound like I picked up with the first woman offering me a shoulder."

Lauren lifted a questioning brow his way. "That's not what I inferred. I'm only asking a question. Was Tara's shoulder always available?"

"Tara wasn't interested in me," Jason assured her. "She was just. . ." He seemed at a loss for words.

Lauren rolled her eyes heavenward. Men could be so dense! "She was just in love with you," she finished for him. Waving off the protest she saw brewing, she quickly pressed on. "It's all right, Jason. I accept the fact that you didn't recognize it. Her motive was ill-conceived, an oddball, sort of mixed-up mess. She probably didn't understand it herself."

She watched him lower his head for a moment before looking back up. "Psycho-speculation!"

"Maybe," Lauren offered gently. "Whatever the reason, it drove her to do what she did." She was amazed at her own relative calm. "But do you really think she was sorry?"

He hesitated. "I always thought so. But you've brought question to that, haven't you?" His brows drew together. "I still don't understand the missed phone call. I can't even begin to fathom what it means. But for right now, I have to believe she made a true decision for Christ." There was a terrible, tense silence before he continued. "You can't know what the thought does to me—"

"No, I can't," Lauren responded, touching his hand lightly. They were quiet for several seconds. "Do you remember what I said to you the day I left?"

He lifted his quizzical gaze, a smile tugging at the corners of his mouth. "Quite a few things, if I remember right."

She smiled back. "I told you the truth always has a way of coming out. It may take a day, a month, or years, but it always comes out." She tugged at his hand. "It was true then, it's true now. If there's one thing I've learned through this ordeal, it's that God does things in His own time and in His own way. We have to trust He knows what He's doing."

"You almost lost that truth because of me," he stated ruefully, shaking his head in self-reproach. "I'm glad you gained your faith back."

Lauren's head shot up. "What do you mean?" How could he know of the spiritual struggles, the struggles that nearly drowned her?

Jason seemed to take great care with his words. "I told you earlier, I've kept some track of you through the years."

Lauren couldn't decide if she should be elated or angry. The memory of the glossy photos came to mind; he'd spied on her before. "But why?"

"I never stopped caring about what happened to you," Jason answered casually.

Lauren had no problem reading between the lines. Caring about what happens to someone and caring for them were two different things entirely. She nodded and stood up. "Just like one of your lost lambs." Just like Tara! She began to slowly gather the plates but stopped. "If you've kept track of me, why didn't you contact me? Things might have turned out differently if you had."

"I'd planned to," he admitted, also standing. "But one thing led to another, and the thing with Tara's phone call wound my clock pretty good. I wasn't sure I even wanted to see you again." He paused. "And there were other things to consider."

Lauren dumped the forks and knives on the tray. "Such as?"

"Well," he hesitated, "there's Tom for one thing. You weren't exactly unattached—"

"Jason!" Lauren nearly cried. "You really have been spying on me!"

"I wasn't spying!" Jason refuted calmly.

"Of course you weren't." Lauren humphed at him and took up the tray. "You're really the limit, Jason Levitte."

Jason only smiled. "I told you this would start an argument!" He picked up the glasses and started for the door in front of her. "I've had enough serious conversation for one afternoon. We have better things to do. You said you wanted to go shopping. Why don't we get ready?"

Lauren stuck her tongue out at his retreating back. *The man has his nerve. He'd known about Tom all along. But how? He couldn't just drop a bomb like that and then change the subject.*

"Jason," she began in her no-nonsense tone.

Jason turned for a brief second. "I'm not discussing the matter any further at the moment, except to say, you don't have to worry that pretty little head of yours with visions of me staring in your windows or any other such wild thoughts. I think you know me better than that."

Lauren knew he'd say no more after meeting his determined stare. He was a stubborn man! Everything had to be in the right time and context for him. Yet, she had so many burning questions and so few answers.

They put the food away in silence. Lauren finally locked the front door and joined Jason on the deck.

"Ready?" Jason asked cheerfully.

"Lead on!" She'd play it slow. Some careful thought was needed on her part.

They started down the steps.

The shrill ring of the phone shot through the open windows. Lauren turned briefly, but waved a hand toward the cabin instead. Whoever it was would call back.

❧

"I had a wonderful time," Lauren said as she scrounged through her purse for the front door key. "I think I overspent, though." The afternoon had gone much too fast and not once did an opportunity come in which she could engage Jason into their previous discussion.

"Levitte's Landing will have to be expanded if you keep shopping there," Jason replied, shifting the heavy shopping bags from one hand to the other.

"I know they're in here somewhere," she groaned, still digging deep into the recesses of her handbag.

His own keys jingled as he leaned past her and easily opened the door.

Lauren breathed a sigh of relief as she stepped through the door and dropped her two packages on the end table. "Never could pass up a good sale," she said grinning. Suddenly she spun toward him. "Wait a minute!"

"Yes?" Jason responded, letting the shopping bags from his own hand glide easily to the floor.

"You just opened the door." Her mouth gaped at the thought. "You have a key to the cabin!"

Jason only shrugged his shoulders, nonplussed. "I found it on the deck when you left here five years ago."

Lauren thought back for a moment. He was right. She'd left it on the table and meant to give it to Tilly, but Jason's appearance had rattled her.

"I'll give it back if it bothers you," Jason continued.

Lauren blinked once. "I don't suppose it matters," she finally said.

"It's up to you," he said in a carefree tone, fingering the key in question. "If it makes you uncomfortable, I can give it back."

"Let's not worry about it right now," she answered, waving him off. For some inexplicable reason, she didn't want the key back. There was an odd security in knowing he'd kept it on his key ring all these years.

"If you change your mind," he continued on, "let me know." He looked at his watch. "I need to go now, but I'll be back in the morning—about nine—to nail down those loose shingles on the gable ends."

"You're leaving?"

Jason grinned. "For now. I have a few things of my own to tend to." He rubbed his chin. "Why? You don't want me to go?"

Lauren met his gaze. No, she didn't want him to go, but she wasn't about to let him know it. And he was being deliberately provocative. "No, that's fine. I have plenty of things to attend to myself."

He smiled knowingly. "All right, then." He leaned forward, giving her a quick peck on the cheek. "Until tomorrow." There was a slight pause.

Lauren braced herself for more, dreading and hoping, but it never came. Instead, Jason let the screen door thud softly behind him. The faint sound of whistling and echoing footsteps across the wooden boards followed him out. She stood stock-still until the musical strain drifted off into oblivion.

# nine

Lauren stared intently at the winding road long after Jason's car had disappeared from sight. Familiar forest sounds comforted then eluded her. Even the wing-clacking crescendo of the summer locust nearly went unnoticed in her absorption. What was she to do? Thoughts tumbled over each other until they drifted to the top like lottery balls, random and out of sequence. Jason had been right about her need for a well-ordered world. She'd denied it then, but in retrospect it made sense. Security and order allowed her to function. Flexible Jason would never understand that. Or maybe it was she who didn't understand Jason.

The sudden ring of the phone broke the spell, and Lauren jerked. An exasperated sigh escaped as she hurriedly entered the cabin and gave a nervous glance at the clock. She'd forgotten Tom—again! Hesitantly she reached for the receiver.

"About time you answered," greeted a booming female voice. Lauren exhaled a breath of relief as her sister, Cassie, continued on in her usual exuberant style. "I've been trying to reach you all day. Where have you been?"

Lauren smiled at her younger sister's bluntness. "I'm on vacation," she answered without remorse. "I was out shopping with Jason."

"Jason?" Her sister gasped, and Lauren could almost imagine her astonished look. "You can't be serious! You're on speaking terms with the man?"

Cassie was the brutally candid one, a trait Lauren both admired and hated. "Cassie," she slowly warned.

"Don't Cassie me!" she retorted. "Have you lost your mind? I don't understand how—"

"You don't have to understand," Lauren interrupted firmly.

Cassie ignored her. "Does Tom know about this?"

"Tom's the one who suggested it."

Silence from Cassie was rare, and Lauren capitalized on it.

"And I didn't call you earlier to talk about my shopping excursion with Jason," Lauren continued.

"The whole world's gone crazy," Cassie muttered.

Lauren couldn't suppress a smile. "I won't argue that fact."

"Well, the message you left on my answering machine sounded so cryptic. I knew something must be up," Cassie parried. "It has to be Jason! You should know being around him again is bound to bring trouble—"

"There's nothing wrong," interrupted Lauren again. Cassie had been Lauren's staunch defender when the trouble began on Bay Island, effectively building dislike for Jason in the process. It was evident Cassie's feelings hadn't diminished in the least. "I just called to ask you a question."

There was caution in Cassie's voice. "All right. What is it?"

"I found out a few days ago that Tara may have tried to call me, maybe about two years ago," Lauren began to explain. "She evidently spoke with someone—"

"That's right! She did!" Cassie broke in. "She spoke with me."

A queasy lump formed in Lauren's throat. "You spoke with Tara?"

Cassie went on undisturbed. "Yes, I spoke with her. I let her know in no uncertain terms her apology was a little too late and a little too phony."

"You didn't!" Lauren cried in disbelief. "Why didn't you tell me?"

There was a sigh on the other end of the line. "You'd been through enough, Lauren. It was time to move on. Things were finally beginning to look up for you and Tom. Tara and Jason would have only muddled things for you again. It just seemed best to not mention the call."

"But Tara was dying," breathed Lauren in a near whisper. She stretched the cord and sank into the kitchen chair.

"Dying?" There was a twinge of disbelief in Cassie's voice.

Hadn't Lauren herself expressed disbelief at the notion? Tara's craftiness made one wary, even of the impossible. "Tara had brain cancer and died over a year ago. Jason said she was trying to make her peace with God about what she'd done." Lauren suddenly felt sick at the thought.

Cassie was unconvinced. "She could have made her peace with God without dragging you through the ordeal with her." There was a stifling pause. "I'm sorry if I caused you any trouble. I really didn't think you'd speak with her, anyway." Her voice turned harsh. "You almost didn't survive Tara's interference the first time around."

Lauren gave a deep sigh. She couldn't fault Cassie for her protective instincts, misguided as they were, and regardless, there was nothing Lauren could do about it now. Her eyes focused on the packages sitting on the floor, the ones Jason had carried. Jason! He'd be overjoyed to hear the news—wouldn't he? Tara hadn't lied after all!

"Are you all right?" Cassie asked with concern after a lengthy silence.

Lauren managed a weak laugh. "I was just wondering how I manage to get into these predicaments without ever participating."

"Trouble does seem to follow you," Cassie agreed in all seriousness. "And that's exactly why you should stay away from Jason." She took a deep breath. "You're not trying to renew anything with him are you? I mean, Tom's a great guy and with your luck—"

"Don't worry about me, Cassie," Lauren assured, thinking over her sister's words. Cassie had always fancied Tom. And if Lauren were to admit the truth, Cassie matched Tom much better than she. Cassie would fit in anywhere, including Africa or Brazil. Wasn't that an ironic twist?

Cassie gave what sounded like a snort.

"Everything will work out," Lauren went on. "And I do

appreciate you telling me about the call—and for trying to protect me."

"Promise me you'll be careful. I don't want to see you hurt again."

Her concern nearly brought tears. "I will."

The two sisters spoke for only a few moments longer before Lauren slowly replaced the receiver.

Ugh! Lauren fingered her aching temples. Cassie would be calling back, she was sure of it. Her sister never gave up. Yet, something loomed larger than Cassie's interference. There was no avoiding what had to be done now. Jason would have to be told! Oh, how she dreaded that! Bowing her head, she prayed for wisdom—a ton of it.

*God, how do messes like this get started in the first place? Did I do right when I left Bay Island five years ago? Did I follow Your will? I thought I had. I did what I thought best!* Her head slumped further. *I was innocent, Lord!*

Long meditative minutes pressed on. Lauren looked about the room as her thoughts drifted to Tom. What was she to do about him? She'd not given him the consideration he'd deserved—especially during his important exams. It was becoming quite evident something vital was missing in her heart for Tom. Love wasn't like that.

The truth was, she didn't love him—not the way a woman should love a man. The thought seared her heart. It wasn't fair to Tom. It wasn't fair to her.

Then there was Jason! She'd been living in a fantasy world the past two days with him. But what had she expected? Even if he still cared for her, he'd lived successfully without her for five years, never needing to see her face or hear her voice— not even once. She'd been easily replaced by Tara then and by a raven-haired beauty now—and there may have been more. It was hopeless to think anything positive was on the horizon. One futile tear trickled unchecked down her cheek.

Several minutes melted into the stillness, and the quiet numbed her whirling thoughts. But the silence began to break, gradually at first, then with increasing urgency. *Clomp—clomp—clomp.* Lauren drew her brows together in concern as the echoing footsteps grew closer and closer. She jumped at the loud knock.

"You in there, Girl?" Tilly's boisterous voice carried through the screen door.

Lauren sniffed and swiped her hand clumsily across her face. It was dry. "Come on in," Lauren called, forcing brightness in her voice.

The door swished open, and Tilly lumbered her full figure inside. "Brought you some cookies." She plopped a plastic container of cookies on the table. "Snickerdoodles."

Snickerdoodles! Jason's favorite! Tilly was determined and persistent. The thought added more weight to her already heavy chest, and the wall of tears she'd successfully held off earlier threatened to break loose.

"Whatever is the matter, Girl?" Tilly demanded when she saw Lauren's face. Swiftly she gathered Lauren to her, draping her arm heavily across her shoulder.

The tears could be held no longer. Unable to speak, Lauren could only shake her head despondently. Tilly led her to the couch, snatching several tissues from the box on the end table as they passed.

"Just cry it out," Tilly soothed, thumping Lauren's back encouragingly. "Cry it all out. Then you can tell me what's ailin' you."

Tilly let her have her cry, occasionally handing Lauren more tissues. Several minutes passed before Lauren gave a final wipe of the tissue and loudly cleared her nose.

"I'm sorry," Lauren squeaked out. "I didn't mean to unload like that."

Tilly waved her off. "Don't you worry yourself none about that." She cocked one eyebrow at Lauren. "Trouble between you and Jason?"

Lauren sniffed and nodded. "I talked with Cassie today,

and she told me what I didn't want to hear." She went on to explain the entire miserable affair. "Oh, Tilly," she moaned, "I wish I'd never discovered the truth. At least my life was calm, even if a little boring in Cincinnati." She swallowed. "Now I have to let go of Tom and lose Jason all over again."

"I understand about Tom," Tilly said. "If you don't love the man, you can't marry him. But what's this about Jason? Afraid he'll not understand about the call?"

Lauren shook her head. "It's more than that, Tilly," she answered sadly. "Jason and I—we can't just pick up where we left off. It's been too long—he doesn't love me."

"How can you say such a thing?" Tilly accused. "I've seen him here every day since you've arrived. What's that tell ya?"

Lauren lifted a weak smile. Tilly would never understand. "He's only trying to make up for how he hurt me," Lauren explained. "You know how he is." She hesitated. "And he has someone else, someone he's built the house for."

"What?" Tilly demanded with a laugh. "You mean Becky?"

"Becky?"

"Petite, black-haired woman?" Tilly described and Lauren nodded. "That's Becky Merrill. She's working for Jason over the summer while on pre-field ministry."

Lauren looked up at Tilly. "Missions?"

"The Congo," Tilly confirmed. "And I can't see Jason getting serious with Becky, especially not when she's leaving for Africa in a year." She chuckled. "And you of all people should know God has to call a person to the mission field. You can't just follow on the shirttail of someone who's heard the call."

The irony struck Lauren, and she gave a watery laugh. "Maybe Becky should meet Tom. Finally—a match made in heaven." A frown slipped over her lips. It wasn't really funny, not at all.

"What you and Jason need, Lauren Wright, is a good talking to," Tilly proclaimed. "I always told you Jason was the one for you. I still believe it. And there's been too much time wasted already with this nonsense. If he's got something going with Becky, tell him to break it."

"Tilly!" Lauren exclaimed in shock. "I most certainly will not. I still have a little pride left."

"It's the problem of saving pride that's fed this whole charade for five years. If you want Jason back, go and get him." She waved a hand in the air. "And if Jason's so serious about Becky, I'd be knowin' about it." She pointed her finger lazily at Lauren. "You talk to him—straight! You hear?"

Lauren nodded grudgingly.

"Enough said, then!" Tilly declared. "Now let's break out the cookies, have a cup of tea, and relax a bit."

❧

Dusk was dropping quickly over the cabin when Lauren received Tom's expected call.

"It was a good day," Tom exclaimed about his exam. "Much easier than Saturday's." He paused only long enough to change the subject. "And what about you? How did things go today?"

Lauren was sensitive enough to know this wasn't the time to reveal her recent insights into their doomed relationship. Tom needed a clear mind for his last exam, and she wouldn't spoil that. "There's not been much of a change," she explained, filling him in on only the most mundane of details.

But Tom was more perceptive than that. "Something's wrong."

"There's nothing wrong," she quickly lied, giving a chuckle to prove it. "You worry too much."

"Maybe because there's something to worry about," he said quietly. "Did you know Cassie called me today?"

Lauren swallowed hard. "Cassie!"

"She told me about Tara's phone call," he continued on. "What I'm wondering is—why you didn't mention it."

Lauren felt trapped! Didn't he understand she wasn't at liberty to say—not right now? Before a proper response could be formed, he continued on.

"Maybe I shouldn't have sent you to Piney Point alone," he declared, worry evident in his voice. "It seemed the right choice at the time, but now. . ." He paused. "Maybe I should come up to Piney Point. I could catch the late boat tomorrow after the exam. We could straighten—"

"No!" Lauren cried hastily, immediately lowering her voice. "There's nothing wrong that a good night's sleep couldn't take care of." As tired as she felt, it was as close to the truth as she dared to hope.

"You know I'd come," he insisted.

"I know you would," she said appreciatively. "But let me handle this my way. I'll work it out and be home by Sunday afternoon just like we planned." She left no room for argument, hating the secrecy she knew was truly for his benefit. But the revelation gave her no comfort.

# ten

Lauren barely laid the receiver to rest before it jumped to life again.

"Hello, Lauren."

"Jason?" Lauren held her breath.

"Didn't wake you, did I?"

"Nope." Sleep! What was that?

"I hoped you'd still be up."

"Really?" She smoothed her hair nervously. "Something wrong?"

"Not at all," he assured. "It's just that I've been thinking—"

"Uh-oh!"

Jason gave a pleasing chuckle. "It's not that bad."

"Don't be too sure. Remember, I know how your ideas work," she teased, feeling much lighter and inexplicably pleased at hearing his voice. "Should I sit down?" A satisfied snicker on the other end made her wonder what he was up to.

"Depends," he responded happily. "Where you at?"

"Same place as usual when I'm on the phone," Lauren laughed. "The cord only stretches so far."

"You should get a cordless."

"That's not why you called, is it?"

"Guess not." His buoyant banter slipped away. "It's something more important than that."

"Yes?"

Jason let the moment hang precariously in the air. "What would you think about staying the summer on Bay Island?"

Lauren nearly choked. "Stay the summer! What are you talking about?"

"I mean, staying on the island for awhile," he answered pragmatically. "I could always use another accountant. We could work something out—"

"I already have a job," she interrupted. Jason was asking her back!

"I know that. Arrangements can always be made with the university. They can live without you a couple months, can't they? And I'd pay for your leave!" he offered, undaunted. "Then, if and when you decided to go back, your job would still be there." He seemed to have the entire scenario mapped out and analyzed. "You can stay right there at Piney Point. The roof and a few other odds and ends need fixing, but I'll get that done tomorrow. The place will be good as new."

This was the old, logical Jason she once knew. The one who thought through every detail, every question, every possibility. All but one question! "Why, Jason?"

"Why, what?"

Lauren rolled her eyes in exasperation. "Why do you want me to stay the summer?"

"It's not obvious?"

"Not exactly." *Say it!*

Silence begged to be relieved before he spoke what she desired and needed to hear. "I don't want you to leave, Lauren." A husky quality crept into his voice. "Seeing you again has just—just made me crazy. I've missed you!" Lauren didn't dare breathe as he continued. "You do something to me, something I can't explain. I'm not wrong in assuming you still feel something too, am I?"

Tingles ran down her spine. Slowly, she chose her words. "There's still something there," she admitted. "I just don't know what it is."

She heard him give an elaborate sigh of relief. "Stay the summer then! Give us the time we need to find out. I don't want us to live our lives in regret over what might have been."

He made it sound so easy, so possible. "But I can't just make a decision like that so quickly!" she countered guardedly, finally stretching the phone cord far enough for her to sink into the kitchen chair.

Jason acknowledged her concern. "It's a lot, I know." His voice softened. "But it's too important to turn down without serious consideration. Will you think it over? Sleep on it?"

What did the man have against sleep? How could anyone sleep with such an issue on their mind? "Do I have a choice?"

He gave a gentle laugh. "Not any more than I do."

"I'll give it some thought," she reluctantly agreed. "But please don't push me if the answer's no."

What he asked seemed exhilarating, yet impossible, totally impossible. Besides, Tom was expecting her back. And as easy as Jason thought her job could be dropped, he didn't understand the weight of her responsibilities. Supervisors didn't just take several weeks off when the whim hit. And Jason had yet to hear the story of Cassie and Tara's phone call. Would the offer be so attractive when he knew? Would he believe her?

"There's one other thing you should know," Jason said softly, breaking into her thoughts.

Uh-oh! Here drops the other shoe. "Yes?"

"We've been through some rough times. I take full blame for that." Lauren lowered her forehead to her palm, resting her elbow on the table as she listened. "No matter about the unexplained call, no matter about what the future holds—I trust you. I believe in you."

A lump was quickly forming in her throat. She couldn't trust her voice to respond. He'd said it! He believed her, even beyond the odds. Her heart quivered.

"And, Lauren?"

"Hmm?" She barely managed a sound.

"I'm going to pray hard about this. You won't make this decision without a lot prayer, will you?"

Didn't he know since her arrival, prayers flowed frequently—in near panic? Not since that last glimpse of Bay Island five years ago had she poured her heart out to God in such torment.

"I'll pray."

"I can't ask for more than that." His voice softened further. "And, Lauren—"

"Yes."

"Sweet dreams!"

❧

The sun woke Lauren early the next morning. For several minutes she lay watching the skittering sunbeams bounce across the ceiling. Tuesday! She glanced at the clock. Jason would be arriving in less than an hour to fix the roof. The thought drew both hope and dread. Slowly she ambled out of bed, showered, and towel-dried her hair, all the while pondering what the day might bring. Could it be there was hope? Into the wee hours of the morning, she'd wondered. But with God all things were possible, right? Would Jason hold true to his convictions of trusting her after she explained Cassie's story? Her thoughts progressed little more before the phone rang.

"Miss Wright?" asked an unfamiliar voice.

"Yes."

"This is Becky Merrill, Mr. Levitte's secretary."

Lauren stood stock-still. The raven-haired beauty! "Yes?" Her voice now held caution.

"Mr. Levitte," the woman began, "asked me to call and let you know he won't be able to keep his appointment with you this morning."

"Appointment?"

"Yes," Miss Merrill confirmed, her manner unnervingly professional. "He's been called out of state, I'm afraid. He's expected back Friday morning and will reschedule with you then."

Appointment! Reschedule! What was happening? "When did he leave?" Lauren asked.

There was hesitation on the other end. "He hasn't left yet," Miss Merrill answered slowly. "But we'll be leaving shortly to make the nine o'clock flight."

The plural emphasis wasn't lost on Lauren as she looked at her watch in disbelief. It was nearly nine now. "He's flying from Bay Airport!" Lauren stated, rather than questioned, in amazement.

"Yes," she answered. "And I'm really sorry to have to cut you short, but we are running late—"

"Thank you for calling, then," Lauren managed to say before numbly resting the phone back into the base.

Unbelievable! How could it be? And why hadn't Jason called himself? What about their day together, their discussion of important issues he never wanted to regret?

A deep breath escaped. Why should it surprise her? Work had always come first, hadn't it? What made her think things had changed on that front? Lauren gave a snort. She supposed he expected her to sit around and wait for him. And she'd be there! There'd be no accusations of her running out this time—no matter the reason.

She couldn't believe Jason was taking a flight from Bay Airport. He'd never done that before. He hated flying in small planes. And small was all the miniature airstrip on the island could handle.

She also mulled over Becky Merrill's words. Was Lauren no more than an appointment to reschedule? She wondered if Jason had led Becky to believe their relationship was all business. Maybe Tilly had missed the mark with Jason and Becky. Had Lauren misunderstood Jason last night? Her heart shriveled at the thought.

❧

The day dragged endlessly until late afternoon when Lauren spotted Larry Newkirk's police cruiser rolling up the incline toward the cottage. He slowed the car to a stop and stepped out. Lauren descended the steps to greet him.

"Brought your necklace," he announced, unfolding his lanky frame from the car. A smile stretched across his boyish face as he leaned into the car to retrieve a small red bag.

"I can't believe you found it," Lauren gushed appreciatively when he passed the bag to her. The crackling plastic bag fell quickly away as she stripped off the soft tissue paper inside to reveal a shiny cross necklace. She lifted the shimmering chain up for inspection. "I don't know how to thank you."

"You don't have to," he responded graciously, watching her delight. "I was just glad to find it."

Lauren gave him a warm smile. "It means the world to me." She unclasped the chain to put it on.

"Here." Larry quickly took the necklace from her fingers and placed it gently around her neck. "There you go."

"Oh, it's beautiful," she exclaimed.

"Yes, it is."

Lauren looked up at him, his uniform badge flashing a slice of sun at her. "Can you stay a few minutes?" she asked, stepping sideways from the glare. "Maybe some lemonade and cookies—"

Larry looked at his watch. "Sorry. I'm on patrol this afternoon."

"That's too bad." She fingered the gold cross. There had to be a way to repay this man's kindness.

"But I'm off in two hours," he said, obviously noticing her disappointment. "Maybe you'd like to take an early supper at Phil's? He still has the best show of fish on the island."

Lauren brightened. "That'd be great." The last thing she wanted to do was mope around until Jason returned. "And I'm buying. You can tell me all about how you found the necklace."

He smiled warmly. "Sounds good. How about six o'clock?"

"Six o'clock it is."

❧

It was well after midnight before the dark blue truck halted in front of Piney Point.

"All these years I never knew those caves existed," Lauren said in astonishment. "I still can't believe it. They're wonderful."

Larry seemed to share her enthusiasm. "We could explore the caves sometime when it's light if you want."

"Even in the daylight, the openings would be hard to find unless you knew they were there."

Larry had driven her to the island's south corridor after dinner to watch the magnificent sunset. It was then he showed her the deeply recessed caves below a treacherous cliff. Larry knew the less perilous route to get a good view.

"With the openings so well hidden, it was a good refuge for criminals," Larry explained.

"I can see why," she replied, stifling a yawn. "It must be getting late. I'm sorry for keeping you out so long. Guess I didn't realize the time."

"I'm a big boy now," he said with a laugh. "With great company, great food, and great scenery, time gets away, doesn't it?"

After viewing the outer caves, it seemed natural to soak up the peace and quiet. Tourists didn't venture much to the less populated southern tip of the island. Water lapped at the shore as they sat on two large rocks, talking amiably. They spoke of the past and then caught up to the present. Larry had graduated from Ohio State University with a law enforcement degree the year before. He wanted nothing more than to stay on the island all the way through retirement.

Larry stifled his own yawn before hopping out of the truck and circling to her door. She stepped out when he opened it.

"Do you need an escort to the door?" he asked, looking up at the cabin.

Lauren glanced at the dark windows. "No. If you'll just wait long enough to see I'm safely in, that'll be fine."

Larry opened the driver's door. "I had a great time," he said, leaning partially out the window opening, a lopsided grin plastered on his face.

Lauren returned the smile. "I did too." It did feel good to

get out—even in her exhaustion, but for that very reason, she was thankful Larry didn't seem inclined to stick around. "Thank you for the lovely evening."

"Anytime," he returned easily. Lauren gave a friendly wave and was about to ascend the steps when he called again. "I noticed earlier the roof could use some nailing on those gable ends." He was pointing toward the roof.

Lauren looked at the roof, remembering Jason's broken promise. "Well—"

"I'll be by in the morning to fix it," he declared, giving Lauren no chance to protest. "I'm off duty tomorrow, and it won't take but a minute."

"Well—"

"Go on up," he said, giving her a verbal nudge. "I'll see you in the morning."

Lauren gave a resigned shrug as she climbed the wooden steps and finally turned the key in the lock. She switched on the porch light and gave an acknowledging wave after entering. She heard the truck's engine start and watched as Larry threw a wave out the window. He soon disappeared into the darkness.

After locking the door securely, Lauren leaned back against it. Jason had been right about Larry. He wasn't a kid anymore, he was a man. The lanky teenager had become a successful and interesting person. She'd enjoyed his company immensely—a platonic and uncomplicated relationship. It was crazy of Jason to think beyond that. A platonic friendship was a precious commodity right now.

With a sleepy smile, she headed off to bed.

# eleven

By eight the next morning, the rhythmic sound of a hammer penetrated her slumber. Blinking sleepily, she swung her legs from the bed and padded over to look out the window. Larry's truck was parked outside and an aluminum ladder leaned at an angle against the front gutter. A smile lit on her lips. At least her parents' cabin was receiving a good overhaul during her visit.

Quickly she showered and dressed before heading to the kitchen. With the flip of a switch and new ingredients, the coffee-maker sputtered to life. She set out two mugs and ambled off to the front room. Cool, fresh air rushed in through the open windows when she pulled open the front door. The screen door creaked as she stepped out onto the porch.

Larry peeked over the edge of the roof. "Finally awake, sleepyhead?"

"I'm on vacation, remember?" she retorted with a smile, using a hand to shield her eyes from the bright sun.

He laughed. "Haven't you ever heard 'the early bird gets the worm'?"

"Sorry! Don't eat worms."

"Glad to hear that," he teased. He disappeared for a second, repositioning his legs. His blond head became visible again. "It won't be much longer. I'm almost done."

"Would you like some coffee? It's fresh and hot."

"Won't turn that down for sure," he laughed. "Give me five minutes."

Lauren nodded and stepped back inside as the hammering resumed. Slowly she poured herself a cup of coffee, all the while trying to smother a yawn. She felt exhausted. The past few days of emotional upheaval and the previous night's late hour were taking their toll. After one sip, she stared into the steadily rising steam.

Her thoughts wandered to Jason. Where was he? And why hadn't he called? Not that she'd thought much about it last night while sitting under the stars. The shimmering night sky seemed to snatch each worry into its vastness. God's vastness! But the welcome, temporary respite was gone now. Morning brought with it the unresolved remnants of yesterday.

The sound of Larry descending the ladder jostled Lauren back to the present. Hastily she made her way to the coffeemaker and poured another cup. Propping the screen door open with her hip, she brought both cups out and sat at the picnic table. Larry was easing the ladder to the ground. He glanced her way.

"Smells good," he said, unsnapping his tool belt from the downed ladder.

"Would you care for some toast or something to go with it?" she offered. "I might be able to find a muffin or bagel."

"Coffee's fine," he answered with a smile as she handed him the cup. He nodded toward the roof. "You might want to think about a ridge vent for the roof."

"Oh?"

"I had one put in," he went on. "It does a lot to cool things down." His gaze scanned the massive trees. "But I suppose with all the trees you might not need it."

Lauren also looked up at the trees. "The cabin does stay pretty cool with all the shade." She thought of Jason building the warm fire just four days ago. Jason! Everything reminded her of him. She shook off the disturbing thought. "Does the roof look okay?"

He nodded. "Good as new."

"I appreciate you doing this," she responded with gratitude. "Jason was. . ." She stopped.

He tipped his head slightly and took a nonchalant sip. "When's Jason due back from South Carolina?"

South Carolina! Larry knew more about Jason's excursion than she did. Could she be the only one in the dark as to his whereabouts?

"I think he's due back Friday," she finally answered.

He nodded and seemed to mull over her reply. "Well, I know it's none of my business," he began, then paused for an uncomfortable moment as she waited, "but I think you should be careful with Jason."

Funny! That was exactly what Jason had said about him. "So I don't get hurt again?" she finished for him.

"Something like that." He fidgeted nervously with the coffee cup. "You're a great person. You could get any guy you wanted." A blush seemed to rush up his neck. "Even I wouldn't turn down the chance. . ."

Oh, no! This wasn't good—or platonic—at all. "That's really sweet to say," she finally mumbled, giving serious thought to what she should say. "And I know you're just being kind. No young man would waste his time on an old fogy like me. Too many girls your own age to choose from." Hint, hint!

He took the cue. "Just be careful, all the same."

Lauren quickly changed the subject. "Now, I'd like to pay you for mending the roof."

"Sorry! Your money's no good with me," he stated, setting down his coffee. He picked up his tool belt. "Matter of fact, I can't even stay to enjoy a second cup. I'm headed over to the church to hang drywall."

"But I've got to do something," she protested. What if she'd hurt his feelings? Had she been too rough, sloughing off his attentions?

Larry hoisted the ladder to one broad shoulder and laughed. "I suppose if you insist, you could treat me to some ice cream after church tonight."

Evidently he'd recovered faster than anticipated. What was she to do?

"Don't worry," he called over his shoulder as he tied the ladder to the side rail of his truck. "I know where you stand. I'm too young for you." He flashed a mischievous smile. "Can't blame a guy for trying, though." He tucked the dangling orange rope from the extension between the rungs. "I'm satisfied with being friends if you are."

The tension deflated like an unplugged inner tube. "Ice cream would be wonderful."

Another smile flickered. "Want me to pick you up?"

"I suppose that'd be best," she answered after some thought. It would be illogical for them both to drive. Prayer meeting! She hadn't even planned to go earlier. Not with Jason gone.

Larry opened the truck door and climbed in. "Great! I'll be by to pick you up at six-thirty."

Lauren waved and turned back to the cottage. She hoped seeing Larry after church was the right decision. Even though he seemed to understand and promised to be just friends, she couldn't bear the thought that this might lead to something awkward. Regardless, she was lonely and looked forward to keeping occupied for the evening. Friday was already approaching with enough trepidation. Jason hadn't phoned during his absence, and she wondered if he'd be back as planned. What if he didn't come back before Sunday? Right now it was becoming hard to distinguish between the hurt and anger she felt at his betrayal, for that's what it was—betrayal. He'd vowed to make things up to her! But where was he? Doing business— always business.

&

The hot sun bore down as Lauren hiked up the narrow trail leading to Tilly's cabin. A cool lake breeze rustled the leaves and kept the temperature bearable. Tilly had called, inviting her for an afternoon visit, quickly reminding Lauren she had yet to visit the familiar cabin she so adored as a child.

The log cabin came into view, and Lauren instantly smiled. The rustic scene blanketed her with its welcome. It was so peaceful and serene. Slowly she stepped up to the covered patio. A white porcelain pitcher and bowl, filled with water, seemed to wait for someone to wash in front of the aging, mounted mirror. The scene took her back to a more pleasant time. A time she wished could be recaptured like an old classic movie tape to be played over and over again.

She tapped the screen door. The wooden frame banged loosely against the doorjamb.

"Tilly?" she called into the screen, her voice echoing back from the windowpane. The scratchy view of the polka-dotted tile floor and well-worn furniture was the same as it was her first summer at Piney Point.

"Is that you, Girl? Come on in. I'm in the kitchen."

The door opened easily as Lauren let herself in. The smell of fresh-baked bread immediately accosted her. "Oh, that smells good," Lauren greeted, savoring a deep breath as she watched the older woman pull two loaf pans from the oven.

"You like it, huh?" Tilly chuckled knowingly.

Lauren nodded. A large paddle fan dispersed the oven heat and wonderful aroma, giving her nose a full and delicious assault.

Tilly straightened and plopped each pan on a cooling rack. "Stollen bread!" she announced.

"Tilly!" Lauren exclaimed in disbelief. "You're baking that for Jason, aren't you?"

The older woman gave a mischievous smile. "What's makes you say that?"

"Because you know very well how much Jason loves your German breads," she scolded. "Just like his favorite pop and snickerdoodles cookies." She couldn't hold back a small smile. "You're really shameless, you know that?"

Tilly only shrugged her shoulders. "Nothin' wrong with makin' someone happy."

"And Jason's not even here to appreciate all your hard work."

"I know that," she answered gaily. "When's he comin' back? Tomorrow?"

"Friday—I think."

Tilly gave her a sharp glance. "He hasn't called?"

Lauren shook her head. "And knowing him, he probably won't. Not when he's caught up with work." She hoped the bitterness wasn't too evident.

But Tilly missed nothing. "Did you have that talk you promised?"

"We did," Lauren answered quickly.

"Well?"

"He was called away before we finished."

Tilly grabbed a pitcher of iced tea from the refrigerator. "You must have got some things straight, 'cause you're not the same wet-eyed girl I left the other day."

Tilly wasn't about to give up. Lauren knew this as well as anything. "He asked me to stay the summer."

"Really!" The pitcher nearly dropped to the counter. A smile split the woman's wrinkles clear in two. "That's wonderful."

Lauren only shrugged. "I don't know. There's a job to think about, my family—"

"And Jason traipsin' off at the drop of a hat," Tilly concluded. She opened the cupboard and reached for two tall glasses. "And you're upset with him!"

"That's part of it," Lauren admitted, holding each glass in turn as Tilly poured the iced tea. "Jason says he's not married to the business, but he really is." She spooned sugar into her glass, giving it an aggressive stir. "He didn't even have the courtesy to call me personally. His secretary did it." The memory still rankled her. "She wanted to reschedule my appointment. Can you believe that?"

Tilly's eyebrows inched up, and she stroked her chin thoughtfully. "Mighty curious."

"I'm trying to give him the benefit of the doubt, but. . ."

Lauren was still vigorously stirring the iced tea. Tilly patted her hand and said, "You're gonna stir the color right out of it, Girl."

"Sorry!" Lauren pulled a yellow napkin from the rooster-shaped holder and laid the spoon on it.

"You know what I think?"

Lauren knew the answer would come regardless of her response. She waited.

"It's time to stop being so self-absorbed." Tilly stared at Lauren for a moment. "Jason is a businessman. He shoulders a lot of responsibility trying to keep his company profitable. A good woman could help him, side up with him—join him."

Lauren stiffened. "What about my dreams? Why can't he side up with me?"

Tilly paused long enough to get two plates, then began cutting one of the loaves of warm bread. Back and forth the knife cut, slowly driving Lauren crazy. Why did Tilly always screech conversations to a halt? One piece of bread fell forward revealing the colorful fruit inside.

"Butter?" Tilly shoved the butter dish toward her, ignoring her look of frustration.

"Why not!" Lauren knew Tilly wouldn't have her say until she was ready. The butter melted over the thick slice, and she took a bite.

"Do you even know what your dreams are, Girl?"

Lauren looked up to see Tilly leisurely buttering her own piece of bread. "I have plenty of dreams."

"Really?"

"Yes, really." She had dreams. Plenty of them. So why couldn't she think of any at the moment?

"Well," she fumbled, "I'd like to be head CPA someday at the university or maybe even teach a couple accounting classes." She racked her brain for more. "It'd be nice to go back to school and get my masters."

"What else?" Tilly encouraged.

"Teach Sunday school again."

"Okay! What else?"

*The woman just doesn't give up!* Lauren smiled. "You know what I'd really like to do?"

"What?"

"I'd like to buy one of those tent trailers and travel to all the state parks." As a child Lauren would sneak over to Uncle Ed's Campground and mingle with the kids at the playground. Food cooking in cast iron pots over smoky fires fascinated her just as much as the tiny houses on wheels. She'd vowed to own one someday, yet hadn't thought of it in years.

"What else?"

Lauren laughed. "All those aren't enough?" She thought harder. "I wouldn't mind having a house with enough land for a little garden. Maybe some tomatoes, corn, peppers. . .and some lettuce." She smiled. "And while I'm dreaming, one of those easy garden tillers would be nice."

"Those are nice dreams." Tilly cut another piece of bread. "Now, do you know what Jason's dreams might be?"

Lauren was taken aback. "I don't know. I suppose all his dreams rest on making his business a success. He doesn't have time for much else."

"Do you think it's possible he might pour himself into that business because there's no one to share his other dreams with?" Tilly rested her heavy hand on Lauren's. "He has plenty of capable people who can handle the day-to-day operations. I think he's givin' it a small trial this week, letting go, you know, just to be with you."

Lauren thought a moment. "But he couldn't do it. It lasted a whole day, and he was off and running again Tuesday morning!"

"Maybe." Tilly gave it some thought. "It must have been somethin' mighty serious for him to leave town while you're here."

"He could have called."

A worried expression creased Tilly's brow. "That's the worrisome part. What would keep him from calling? I'm tellin' you, it must have been somethin' mighty important." There was a long silence, and she appeared finished with the interrogation and lecture. "Are you comin' to church tonight?"

Lauren told her of Larry's invitation.

"Nice boy, that Larry is," Tilly said with a nod.

Lauren wanted to tell her that the nice boy had grown into a man, but thought better of it. Tilly didn't need any extra ammunition. She was too good with what she already had.

Tilly kept right on talking. "Everything's gonna work out fine. You'll see!"

Lauren wished she could be so sure. Time was running out, running against her. If God was going to remedy the situation, He'd need to act quickly. But she, of all people, knew God worked on His own timetable.

# twelve

The midnight hour pressed close as Larry rolled the truck to a noiseless stop in front of the Piney Point cottage.

"Safe and sound," he announced with a smile, shutting off the engine. "Hope you had a good evening."

Lauren looked over in the darkness. "If anything, it's been memorable."

He chuckled. "I'll take that as a compliment."

"Mr. Edwards will never look me in the eye again." She chuckled quietly, still recalling the gawking look of surprise behind the old man's thick glasses. "I still can't believe you did that."

Larry smirked. "If I'd known the old guy was supplementing his retirement dipping ice cream at the Dairy Barn, I'd have taken you there sooner."

"But you did everything except pull your badge to shame the man into buying my ice cream!" She'd never admit the tiny inkling of satisfaction she felt.

"He owes you more than a double cone, I assure you." He smiled again. "You noticed he didn't argue."

A laughing gurgle escaped from Lauren. "I wouldn't have argued either. Not with a two-hundred-pound police officer breathing down my neck."

She thought of Jason. How would he have reacted upon seeing Mr. Edwards making milk shakes and cleaning tables? She was sure he would have handled the situation differently, with more finesse, more patience. Jason had compassion for people. He wouldn't have painted Mr. Edwards into a corner as Larry had done. But Larry was young and impulsive. She hoped a few more years would smooth out the rough edges causing such direct action. Larry was protecting her honor and didn't seem to care whether he'd squeezed it from the old man willingly or not.

But Jason hadn't escaped Larry's keen sense of protection either. No amount of assurance on her part seemed to clear Jason of his earlier deeds, those Larry thought unforgivable. Of course, Lauren wasn't entirely convinced herself. That didn't help matters. It was good Larry kept more thoughts to himself than he voiced, yet disapproval remained etched on his features.

"I hope you're not mad about it," Larry went on about Mr. Edwards, seeming genuinely concerned.

"I'm not mad," she reassured. Embarrassed—yes. Pleased— maybe a little. But she suspected God wasn't pleased at all.

"And I've kept you out late again. Guess I owe you another apology for that." His tone didn't sound the least bit apologetic.

"It was well worth it to see the sunset again," Lauren remarked truthfully. She opened the passenger door and stepped down. "And I appreciate the lift to church—and the ice cream." She'd been careful all evening, especially at church where tongues could wag faster than lightning, to keep their conversation and manner low-key. It wouldn't pay to start another scandal. Keeping her own head afloat was hard enough.

Larry lighted from the truck. "You didn't put the porch light on again," he scolded. "You really should to be safe. It's just too dark without it." He followed her to the steps. "I'll walk you to the door."

"I did turn on the light. But like everything else, the bulb must need to be replaced."

"I can change—"

She laughed. "The bulb I can manage."

"All right," he drawled. "But I'll see you to the door all the same."

Lauren quickly ascended the steps with Larry following close behind. Thankfully, he stayed back a comfortable distance as she opened the screen door. It wasn't a decent hour for the man to linger. But all thoughts screeched to a halt as the solid door slowly swung open before the jingling keys hit their mark. Icy fingers of fear grabbed at her heart. She took an involuntary step back.

Larry seemed to sense her fear and stepped forward. "What—"

The phone inside the cottage blared like a siren, nearly causing her heart to stop. Before she could step back further from fright, there was a loud crash. Suddenly, a tall figure loomed alarmingly close before her. Then Lauren felt the forceful blow of the stranger's body as he forced his way past, sending her flying backward over the deck furniture. Chairs scraped loudly across the wood planks and tumbled haphazardly. She heard a man groan, but whether it was the intruder or Larry she couldn't tell. Thunderous footsteps tore down the steps.

She lay stunned, one leg painfully arched over a wrought iron plant stand and the insistent ring of the phone added to the continuing chaos.

"Are you okay?" called a breathless voice.

Relief rained down as she recognized Larry's voice. "Yes," she quickly answered without thought.

Larry's silhouette stumbled forward. "Stay right here," he ordered. His footsteps treaded heavily down the steps, and he disappeared.

Lauren strained to hear over the unrelenting phone as she tried to disentangle her leg from the plant stand and a deck chair. For the first time, pain seared across her right arm as she leaned precariously. She winced hard and bit back the groan forcing its way up her throat.

Shouts echoed through the trees some distance away. Tilly! The voices came from the direction of Tilly's cabin. Lauren pulled the painful arm across her stomach in an effort to sit up, loosing a cry of torment. Her body fell back again, tears of agony squeezing past her tightly closed eyes.

She knew her arm was badly broken.

The phone stopped! Minutes ticked by as she lay perfectly still, the pain easing slightly. The starry sky seemed to stare down upon her pathetic figure sprawled across the deck.

"Jason," she groaned. "Where are you, Jason?"

Silence greeted her.

"I need you, Jason Levitte." It was little more than a raw whisper.

A rifle blast pierced the night.

Lauren jerked and another spasm of pain coursed through her. "Oh, God, please don't let Larry be hurt." The thought of her own helpless state brought a renewed sense of panic. "I'm scared, Father. Please don't leave me."

An eternity seemed to pass before snapping twigs and the whipping sound of weeds against someone's heavy stride grew ominously louder. Lauren stiffened in fear.

"Lauren?" There was a winded desperation to the man's voice. Larry's voice.

No air managed to squeak past her windpipe. He was okay! He hadn't been shot. *Thank You, dear Lord,* she prayed. Two figures emerged from the shadows. Was danger still afoot? Fresh fear gripped her.

"Sit still," Larry ordered the second figure. "I'd just as soon this woman shoot you."

Lauren swiveled her attention to a third person, several yards away. The dark made it impossible to see who it was.

Larry was noisily taking two steps at a time. "Lauren? Are you okay?" Worried concern saturated his every word.

"My arm's hurt," Lauren sputtered. "I think it's bad." Just the act of speaking drew the throbbing ache to new heights.

Larry carefully moved two chairs aside and knelt close. "Just sit tight," he murmured. "I'm going to see if I can get some light." He quickly left her side and headed for the cottage door.

"You'd better not have hurt that girl," a woman's strained voice threatened.

Lauren turned toward the voice as a flood of light illuminated the blackness. Squinting, she saw Tilly jabbing the point of her rifle toward the darkly clad figure.

"Tilly!"

"It's me, Girl," came the reply. "This rascal hurt you?"

Larry was rushing to her side again, his eyes roving over her in quick assessment. A curse spilled from his lips. "You're arm's busted up pretty bad." He didn't touch her, but rocked on his heels in contemplation. "Are you hurt anywhere else?"

Lauren said nothing for a moment as she eyed him. "Don't."

"Don't what?"

"Don't curse."

He was silent for the longest time, and she could tell he was wondering if she was coherent. His worried expression deepened. "Did you hit your head?" He didn't wait for an answer as he cautiously examined her head.

"My head's fine." Lauren nearly laughed, but pain kept the impulse in check. "It's just my arm—I think."

He didn't look quite convinced. "First, we need to get you some help," he announced and stood. "Sit tight."

"I'm not going anywhere," she answered.

"You doing okay, Tilly?" he called, making his way down the steps. He paused only long enough to see her head nod.

"This scoundrel ain't goin' nowhere." Tilly jabbed the rifle at the figure again for emphasis. "Is Lauren hurt bad?"

Larry pulled a cell phone from the truck, angling the keypad to the light. "Looks like one arm took the brunt of it." He dialed the numbers, and his voice lowered. "She might have taken a knock to the head."

His voice wasn't low enough to keep Lauren from hearing, and Tilly's responding grunt certainly echoed loudly enough. Only a snippet or two of the phone conversation, however, reached Lauren. Waning strength drew her interest away anyway. She gave a long and weary exhale, drawing Tilly's attention.

"Tell 'em to get here and quick," Tilly demanded.

Larry stuffed the slender phone into his back pocket. "Help's on the way!"

≈

Jason arrived on an early-morning flight and didn't bother to phone before driving to Piney Point. He parked beside Larry's dew-covered truck, his gaze lingering only a moment on the sight before turning toward the cabin.

A wobbly Lauren stepped sideways out onto the deck, her tall frame leaning heavily against Larry. Her beautiful brown hair was mussed and disorderly—a rarity for Lauren. He'd have found it endearing and attractive if not for her behavior. The pair pivoted toward the steps. It was then Jason saw that her right arm was bandaged and in a sling.

Larry frowned when he saw Jason, then turned his attention back to Lauren. "Just take it slow. That pain medication has you higher than a kite."

Lauren gave an easy, slow smile. "Yeah."

Larry shook his head and glanced at Jason.

"What day is it?" Lauren asked.

"Thursday," Larry answered. "Look, Jason's back a day sooner than expected."

"Oh!"

"Whoa," Larry warned, pulling her back from the top step. "You're going to take a tumble."

Jason didn't wait an extra second before quickly climbing the steps. "What happened?" he asked, looking at Larry first and then Lauren.

"It was terrible, just terrible," Lauren slurred. She broke from Larry's grasp and lurched heavily into Jason's arms, practically knocking him off balance.

Jason looked at Larry in alarm.

"Her arm's broken in two places. It happened during a break-in last night." Larry glanced toward the front door. "We surprised an intruder, and she got knocked down hard."

*We?* Jason wondered.

"I'm fine now," Lauren murmured, smiling up at Jason, apparently oblivious to the serious nature of the conversation.

"No, you're not," Larry countered, then looked at Jason. "She's on some heavy drugs. The urgent care doctor gave her a whole arsenal full." He looked at his watch. "We were just on our way to Mercy Hospital on the mainland where the orthopedist should be waiting to set her arm. That first dose of pain medication will be wearing off soon. Hopefully, it'll last long enough to get her there."

Jason repositioned his bearing as Lauren leaned more weight on him. "I'll take her over."

Larry looked about to argue but shrugged his shoulders instead. "Take her to the emergency room. They're expecting her to check in there. Her insurance card is in her wallet, in case she's still fuzzy when you get there."

Both men helped her into Jason's car.

"Are there any papers from urgent care I need to bring?" Jason asked.

Larry shook his head. "They didn't give me any. Evidently, the doctor already faxed over what they needed."

Jason climbed into the car and rolled the window down. "Did you catch the guy?"

For the first time, Larry smiled. "He's sitting in the tank as we speak."

Silence lingered a moment until Jason spoke again. "Thanks for taking care of her, Larry."

"Yeah, well." Larry seemed at a loss for words.

"Hey, Jason," Lauren interrupted happily. "Larry, here, made old Mr. Edwards give me ice cream."

Jason frowned at her in confusion before looking back to Larry.

"It's a long story." Larry leaned close to the window and gave Jason a meaningful look. "Better get to the ferry before the drugs wear off. This happy side is no comparison to her pre-drug condition."

Jason nodded and turned the ignition key.

"Call me on my cell phone when she gets into surgery, and I'll fill you in," Larry said, nodding toward the deck.

He gave a Larry quick wave and let the car coast down the slight incline. At least the early hour would benefit their travel time.

"It was cookies and cream," Lauren began talking again. "You know I like cookies and cream."

"I know." Jason looked in the rearview mirror at Larry's lone figure.

Lauren kept right on talking. "And did you know there's hidden caves on the island?"

"No, I didn't," he humored, still troubled. "Now, why don't you just lay your head back for a few minutes and rest?"

"But I have so much to tell you," she said wistfully.

Jason looked over at her. "Close your eyes and rest. You'll need all the strength you can muster."

It was going to be a very long journey to the mainland.

# thirteen

An annoying insect threatened to ruin an otherwise perfect nap. Lauren gave it a halfhearted slap as she burrowed her head deeper into the scratchy pillow. She felt so heavy, so sleepy.

"She's coming around," a garbled voice announced.

Couldn't a body get some rest? Lauren forced one eyelid slightly open, but exhaustion quickly dropped it back in place. Sleep, sweet sleep. Approaching awareness, however, drew notice to several uncomfortable sensations. Her throat felt parched, for one, and the pesky bug just wouldn't quit.

"Lauren." The dreamy masculine voice definitely caught her attention.

Lauren ventured another peek. With effort, the double image slowly drew into focus.

"Jason?" she croaked hoarsely, finally recognizing his face so near. The familiar scent of his musky cologne seemed to kiss the air ever so lightly. For one short moment she basked in his presence before questions began to surface. Where was she, and why was Jason with her? Her head twisted uncomfortably to get a better view. Unfamiliar surroundings created further confusion.

"You're still at the hospital," Jason explained, his hand grasping hers through the side rail opening. "Dr. Lazero set your arm, and everything's fine."

Lauren swept her tongue across dry lips. "Hospital?" Snatches of memory began to leak through the cracks of consciousness. The intruder, her fall—the pain. Her eyes closed in reflection. It was coming back. And Jason had arrived early at the cabin, but she hadn't expected him. Not

109

that she'd cared much at the time. Just seeing him seemed to make everything fall into place, all nice and tidy. All she'd wanted was to be held by him. Had she really thrown herself into his arms? That short memory clip seemed clearer than the rest. But the memory faded from there. "What day is it?"

Jason smiled indulgently. "It's still Thursday morning. You've only been out for about half an hour."

A rustling movement sounded from the other side of the bed. "Can you wiggle your fingers for me, Lauren?"

For the first time Lauren noticed the uniformed nurse, a shiny, green stethoscope hung about her neck. "Huh?" She looked down at the white cast hidden under the blue sling. Pale, swollen fingers protruded like tree stubs. She moved them slightly and with great reserve.

"That's good," the nurse encouraged. "The fingers will be stiff for awhile, at least until the swelling goes down." She bent closer for observation, pinching each fingernail. "Are you having any pain?"

Lauren shook her head. "But I could sure use some water."

"Let's start with some ice chips," the nurse responded, taking the chart from the nightstand. "Be right back."

*Ice chips? No, no, no! I want ice water—supersized.*

"Thirsty, are we?" Jason asked, watching her frown.

Lauren shifted her gaze back to him, and the frown lifted slightly. "Yes, we are."

"What's this *we* stuff?" He laughed. "You got a mouse in your pocket?"

She couldn't help but smile. He hadn't used that line on her for ages. It always made him laugh, the delightful laugh she'd so missed. "What time did you say it was?"

He looked at the wall clock. "I didn't say, but it's ten-thirty." His chin rested squarely on the rail. "They said you could leave as soon as the twilight sleep wore off."

The effects of the anesthesia were quickly wearing thin, she could tell. She didn't feel giddy at all, not like she had on arrival. But at least the pain had vanished—a definite blessing after the terrible night she had. And what a night it'd been. She glanced at Jason. Judging by the looks of his disheveled hair, the dark circles under his eyes, and his shadowy beard, he hadn't faired much better.

"You really look terrible," she observed, wondering if he'd gotten even less sleep than she.

His chin dipped further over the rail, and he gave her a lopsided smile. "Thanks! I love you too."

"Funny!"

"It was meant to be." A yawn escaped as his smile deepened.

Despite his tousled appearance, his good humor remained unaffected. And he seemed so innocent and appealing with those compassionate eyes. But caution was needed. She hadn't forgotten his abrupt departure two days before or his failure to call.

"When did you get back to the island?"

He stretched and arched his back like angel wings. "Flew in early this morning." Another yawn.

"Did you fly into the island airport?"

"Yep!"

"But you hate those planes."

"Yep!"

"Why didn't you take the ferry from the mainland then?"

He studied her closely before answering. "Because Lauren Wright was waiting on the island and flying all the way saved a lot of time, time that couldn't be wasted." Suddenly he laid his hand on her good arm; his fingers felt warm on her skin.

Lauren felt a strange thrill of joy accompanied by a surge of perplexity. Had Jason disregarded his own safety in order to be by her side? Had he even known of her need? She remembered crying Jason's name during the most frightening moments of the ordeal as she lay helpless under the dark sky. Yet it made no sense. Why should he rush back to her side when he hadn't even called during his absence?

Such thoughts were abruptly halted when the nurse sauntered into the room with a large cup of ice.

"Dr. Lazero has written your discharge papers," she announced. "We'll see how you do with the ice, and if you feel awake enough, we'll get you signed out." She extended the ice-filled paper cup and a spoon to Lauren. "Take it slow to start," she cautioned.

Lauren accepted the cup and unconsciously looked over at Jason. The nurse's well-put advice, she thought, could apply to more than just the cup of ice.

❧

"The horse-pills are three times a day," Jason read, holding the brown prescription bottle in one hand and balancing the list of hospital instructions against the steering wheel of his swaying car with the other. "Those are the anti-inflammatory drugs."

An abrupt horn blast from the ferry broke loose giving Lauren a start. She stretched her neck to see past the hood to the churning blue water. They were almost to the island. "I'm to take them on an empty stomach, right?" One eyebrow went up in deliberation. "Or was that on a full stomach?" Oh, she'd never remember anything after those mind-boggling drugs the night before.

"The bottle says to eat something before taking the medication to prevent stomach upset," he answered, turning the bottle on end to read the red, vertical pharmacy sticker.

"What's in the other bottle again?"

Jason dropped one prescription bottle into the white paper sack and retrieved another. "These are the pain pills." He gave a mischievous smile. "Not as potent as you're used to, though, I'm afraid."

She ignored him. "And what about the other discharge instructions?"

"Use cold compresses as needed and follow up with Dr. Lazero on Monday."

Lauren glanced over at him. "Cold compresses? Over the cast?"

"Guess so." Jason shrugged. "I didn't even think to ask when she rattled off all those directions."

"And the appointment's Monday?" Surely her mind must have flown south to miss the implication of timing that presented. She would be due back at work on Monday.

"Monday at one o'clock," he confirmed, glancing her way before absently asking, "Is the time a problem?"

"Yes," she answered with a sigh. The boat bumped against the dock with a slight jolt. "I'm supposed to be in Cincinnati by Monday."

He turned toward her, his gaze raised candidly to hers. "I know we haven't fully discussed your staying the summer yet, but I thought with this latest development, you'd at least stay until you're well enough to go back."

With the oddest little thrill running up her spine, she gazed back. It all seemed so simple the way he presented things. Yet it wasn't simple at all. She'd almost considered his offer—until the raven-haired beauty called. Ever since, the pendulum of decision couldn't quite find its center mark. "It's just a broken arm. It'll heal just as well there as here," she reasoned.

"It's not just a broken arm," he argued. "You actually broke two bones and damaged part of a tendon." He looked at her sling with hard speculation. "Not to mention the fact you're right-handed. Work will have to wait either way. And you can't drive while you're on that pain medication."

Her gaze fell to the sling. Jason was absolutely right. "And it also means I can't work for you either," she countered.

"I'll find something for you to do," he assured with a wave of his hand. "Staying at Piney Point solves all your problems. It only makes sense, Lauren." He ticked off three fingers. "You're temporarily out of service for working on a computer, I'm providing the perfect substitute job, and there's someone here who can take care of you."

Trying to examine the situation dispassionately with Jason

by her side was impossible. "I don't exactly need to be taken care of," she muttered. "I can still function."

He eyed her dubiously. "That may be true, but will you feel totally safe at the cabin? What about tonight, tomorrow night?"

Lauren felt the color drain slightly from her face. "Well, Larry did catch the guy," she began unconvincingly, trying to gain a momentum of assurance, more for herself than Jason. "He wasn't even an islander, but a drifter, an oversized juvenile looking for something to steal. It was only a fluke. It won't happen again." But how would she feel when darkness dropped its cloak tonight? Would she feel so safe then? "I suppose I might be a little jittery," she finally admitted. "Who wouldn't? But I'm sure it'll be fine."

The boat ramp dropped loudly against the concrete, and Jason gave her a penetrating look as he started the car. "I'm staying the night, regardless."

"You can't do that," she gasped, growing restless under his gaze. "It's not appropriate."

"Protecting you is quite appropriate." Without looking at her, he steered the car off the ferry. "You weren't alone last night."

Lauren could feel color storming up her face. "That was police business. I can't believe you'd even insinuate—"

"I'm not insinuating anything," he answered calmly. "I know exactly why Larry stayed the night, as well he should have, given the situation." He turned the car toward town and glanced her way again. "I called him from the hospital this morning. We had nice chat."

"Oh, really." She gave him a curious look. "Then he told you how the whole thing happened?"

He nodded. "Larry said you surprised the kid at the door and he bolted, knocking you across the deck as he did."

"The phone spooked him," she quickly added.

"The phone? What time was it?"

"I think it was near midnight or a little after," she recalled after a moment of thought.

"That was me calling."

Lauren lifted one eyebrow a fraction, but didn't dare look at him. "You called?"

"Well, you were never home any other time," he countered. "I was forced to call off-hours, figuring you'd at least be home by midnight." Was there a note of accusation in his voice? "I let it ring for a long time."

"I know." How could she forget the phone that wouldn't quit?

She'd later learned while fighting off her painful condition during those tense moments, Larry had quickly overtaken her clumsy intruder on the path to Tilly's cabin. Then Tilly joined the confusion, sporting a .22 caliber rifle, ready and willing to shoot the criminal with perfect aim. It didn't pay the intruder to be fooled by the woman's age. Her agility and quick thinking were not to be underestimated.

Jason gave her an odd, level look, his gray eyes unreadable. "I figured you just weren't answering your phone."

Lauren looked up in surprise. "Why would I have done that?"

"So you wouldn't have to talk with me," he answered without hesitation. "It seems to me you might be sore about me leaving the island so abruptly."

"I wasn't," she lied nonchalantly, watching his wary eyes scrutinize her face.

"Maybe, maybe not. But even now you seem a bit reserved," Jason observed after a moment of uncomfortable silence. He maneuvered the car to a stop at the curb across from the public park. "It's been especially noticeable since the drugs wore off this morning."

She felt her cheeks blanch again. "I can't be held accountable for anything I said or did while under the influence." The memory was too humiliating.

He chuckled. "All right!" He twisted slightly in the bucket seat toward her. "But I want to clear up the situation, and I think you'll understand the urgency of my departure once I explain.

And I plan to explain right now before we go any further."

"There's no need to explain, Jason." There most certainly was every reason, but she wasn't about to admit how badly she wanted to know.

"I'm going to tell you anyway," he said with determination. "I wanted to call you before I left, but there just wasn't time. We had an emergency at one of the other sites in South Carolina where a dockside shop collapsed."

This drew Lauren's full attention. "A collapse? I didn't even know you had built any other shopping centers."

He nodded and went on. "Two others, actually—Charleston and Fort Myers."

"I had no idea," Lauren responded, then asked with concern, "Was anyone hurt?"

"Thank the good Lord, no," he answered. "It happened in the early morning hours when no one was around except a security guard. But the other stores had to be shut down until the cause could be determined, just in case the collapse was in any way related to the design." Three young children skipped gaily past them, glancing curiously at the idling car before crossing the street toward the park. Jason seemed not to notice. "By the time I got the call, there wasn't much time to locate the job plans, let alone make any phone calls before catching the plane. Nearly missed it, as it was." He let his gaze fall on her. "I didn't have a choice. I had to be there!"

She didn't argue the fact but returned his pointed look. "And what did you find out?" She couldn't imagine the meticulous Jason ever designing anything faulty.

He scowled. "The contractor overran costs and used below-grade materials on the last three shops." There was consolation in his words. "But at least it wasn't the design!"

"I'm glad everything worked out," Lauren responded. She truly felt glad for Jason's sake. Despite her opinion of his workaholic patterns, he deserved better for his hard work. But the raven-haired beauty flashed before her eyes. She'd apparently never get an explanation as to why she was in attendance. Just like she might never know the mystery surrounding the house at Muriel's Inlet.

"I'm just glad to be back," he went on. "And I'm looking forward to the Skipper's Festival this weekend." He threw her a quick glance. "We are still going?"

"Of course."

"Your arm won't bother you?"

"I'm sure it'll be okay."

"And you're not mad about my leaving the island?"

"I told you I wasn't."

Jason's persistence remained as if he detected an unsettled element to their conversation. "Everything's in the open then?"

Lauren hesitated.

"Whatever it is, let's talk about it," he insisted.

"There is something I need to tell you." This was awful. So much had happened; she'd nearly forgotten about Cassie and her admission of guilt—until a few minutes ago. "I spoke with Cassie the other night," she began, pausing long enough to collect her thoughts.

"And?"

Lauren found she couldn't quite look into his gray eyes as the story she'd rehearsed so many times spilled out, every detail she was loath to remember. "I really can't blame her," she finished. "She was just trying to protect me." She watched carefully for any reaction on Jason's part. He gave none. "I know this doesn't look good for me, but it's the honest truth. I had no idea Tara called."

An eternity of silence passed before he spoke. "I'm relieved to know Tara's conversion was real." He seemed genuinely comforted, but not satisfied. "And I believe you, Lauren." He paused again in thought. "But there's just one thing I can't but wonder."

"Yes?"

"Was Cassie protecting you from Tara—or from me?"

Lauren thought the question over a moment. "Both," she answered with brutal honesty. "Things were really going well for me by that time, and Cassie didn't want to see me hurt again. She's leery of you even yet."

Jason nodded and fingered the keys dangling from the ignition. "And what about you? Do you think I'm a threat to your stable life?"

Not sure how to respond, Lauren didn't answer right away. "What's that have to do with Cassie and the phone call?"

"Didn't say it had anything to do with the call," he said quietly. "But you've said all along Tara did what she did to protect me—from you. Now you say Cassie's done what she's done to protect you—from me." Even though his voice held steady, Lauren could hear the pain in his words. "I just want to know if you feel the need to be protected from me."

He seemed genuinely taunted by the possibility, and Lauren felt a tug deep in her soul. "In a way, you do pose a threat," she admitted softly. "Just coming back to Piney Point, seeing you again, and facing God's command to forgive, have literally pulled the rug out from under me." Lauren drew in a deep breath. "Just when I think I've come to grips with you and this forgiveness thing, I lose it again." Nervously she fingered the hem of her blue sling. "But I'm learning and coming closer to it than I have in the past five years."

"But there isn't much time, now, is there," he stated matter-of-factly. "You're still planning to leave Sunday?"

How could she answer what she didn't know? It made perfect sense to stay on, at least for a short time until things settled. Yet, she hadn't even talked with Tom, not about their doomed relationship, nor the chaotic events surrounding her now.

"I can't commit either way just yet," she finally answered, a sudden weariness overtaking her.

"I'll take that answer—for now," he said, putting the car in gear before easing back into traffic. "But I can be persistent."

How well she knew!

# fourteen

Several parked cars crowded the area surrounding the cabin at Piney Point causing Jason a bit of tight maneuvering to press his large car in close.

"Where did all these cars come from?" Lauren wanted to know, alarmed at the sight. Thoughts of the jimmied front door left unrepaired that morning opened several possibilities for disaster.

Jason turned the ignition off, looking perplexed as well. "Larry said some church folks might be bringing food, but it shouldn't take this many people to bring over a casserole or two." He paused at the sound of an electric drill and hammering wafting from the cabin's open door. "Well, at least we know two people are fixing your busted door."

Lauren reached over with her left hand to unlatch the passenger door. "We'd better see who is here." The thought of people, especially church people, milling about inside her cabin rooted an unsettled feeling.

"Wait and I'll open your door," Jason commanded, hopping out quickly. He opened her door. "Can you make it?"

Deep bucket seats made twisting her body difficult without the aid of her right arm. "I can do it," she assured, resolutely rocking her weight forward enough to gain the proper momentum. A slight, but audible grunt escaped as she successfully extricated herself. "Could you please get the prescription bag? It's on the floor."

She moved out of the way as Jason leaned into the car and retrieved the white paper bag. He closed the door just as Tilly came bounding out of the cabin, across the deck, and down the steps.

"Where've the two of you been?" Tilly asked happily, gently patting Jason on the cheek before sidling up to Lauren. "We've been waitin' with a fine spread of food." She eyed Lauren's sling. "Did you make out okay at the hospital?"

Lauren nodded, her attention still riveted to the cottage where voices mingled with the sound of power tools. Any hope for a quiet afternoon seemed distant.

Tilly nudged them forward. "Come on! The ladies are fixin' up the place." She looked at Jason, a frown crinkling her brow. "That rascal sure did make a mess."

The cottage had been in disarray after the burglary, but Lauren's euphoric condition hadn't allowed for the least bit of worry. Now the memory of strewn books and overturned drawers drew a troubled sigh.

"Does it look like the guy took anything?" Jason asked as they walked.

"Hard to tell." Tilly started up the steps first. "There was some jewelry, but Larry got it back, probably holdin' it for evidence."

Lauren stopped mid step, her hand flying to her throat. "My cross necklace!"

"I'm sure Larry has it," Jason reasoned, his light hold on her good arm tightening with reassurance. "But we'll take a look here first to make sure."

Tilly made it to the top step. "Don't worry none about that. Larry nearly turned that scoundrel upside down to empty his pockets. You'll get it back."

Lauren didn't doubt Larry made an aggressive search, but she wouldn't rest until the necklace returned safely to her very own hands.

"Here they come," called a voice from the screen door. Lottie Bon Durant opened the squeaky screen door to let Tilly and the couple in. Wood splinters and dust littered the entryway.

Lauren managed a smile as she passed through. Two church deacons and several ladies, many in work smocks, swarmed the living room. Dishes of food loaded the small dining table like an oversized smorgasbord, and delicious smells permeated the room. Everyone seemed to be speaking at once.

"I don't know what to say." Overwhelmed, Lauren surveyed each hopeful face in turn. "This is wonderful." The place was spotless—with no sign of the disturbance she'd experienced. The welcoming smells of home flooded the place. The kindness evident here soothed her bruised soul. Yet, guilt seized her. Those earlier, ungrateful thoughts she held against her brothers and sisters in Christ were straight from the pit of Hell, and she knew it. These God-fearing people, like herself, were capable of making errors of judgment and needed her forgiveness as much as she needed theirs. How many times would God need to forgive her before she understood the dynamics of such actions? The thought made her reel in wonder, and she found herself swaying ever so slightly.

Jason put his arm around her waist, steadying her, and took over. "Let's give Lauren a little room," he told the well-wishers with a smile. He turned to her. "Do you need to freshen up and maybe look for your necklace?" She nodded absently, and he turned his attention to the others. "Give us a few minutes, and we'll be back to dig into that great food."

The ladies smiled appreciatively as Jason threaded Lauren through the crowd toward the back hall. Immediately the ladies busied themselves with final food preparations.

"Are you doing okay?" he asked with concern as they entered the back room, his arm still firmly wrapped around her.

Lauren met his eyes. "I'm afraid the effects of the medication last night haven't totally worn off yet." She couldn't tell him his close presence made her head spin much more than any drug ever could, and for the moment she didn't want to think about the raven-haired beauty, his mystery house, or any other unresolved issues. How nice it would be to cut loose those strings and love the man as she had so many years ago, as her heart wanted to do at this very moment.

Jason led her to the white wicker chair situated between the bed and window, and quickly brought over the wooden jewelry box. "Take a look and see if your cross necklace is there."

Lauren fingered the latch and slowly lifted the pine cover, drawing a soft gasp upon seeing dirty smudges speckled across the empty red velvet bottom. "It's gone," she whispered. "It's all gone." Weary dismay overtook her. The creep not only took her most precious life mementos, but touched her things with grimy hands, leaving a frightening scent of desecration in his wake. In one lone night, her security and sense of well-being had been stripped away.

"Larry probably has your jewelry in evidence as Tilly said," Jason said logically, dropping on one knee beside her. Softly he lifted her chin with his fingers. "I'll make sure you get the necklace back." Gray eyes searched hers. "I hate to see you like this." He pulled her close to his chest, his voice vibrating against her ear. "I'd have done anything to have protected you from this."

Lauren closed her eyes for fear she'd cave in to the growing urge to cry, something she definitely didn't want to do. Her tired mind needed some sleep, and a good shower and afternoon nap would restore the energy needed to keep things in perspective.

"Let's get something to eat," Jason said after several silent moments ticked away. He placed the jewelry box back on the bureau. "I don't know about you, but I'm starved."

"Oh, Jason. I didn't even think," Lauren replied aghast. "You've been up all night and haven't even had breakfast or lunch."

Jason chuckled. "By the looks of the food laid out on your dining room table, it was worth the wait."

"All that food! Can you believe it? It's enough to feed an army!" she exclaimed, still amazed by the women's generosity. She stood, catching a glimpse of her unkempt appearance in the wall mirror. Dark circles accented her wide eyes, and she stared at her pale reflection. Her hair pressed into unnatural waves of dull brown chaos. What a mess!

Jason drew her away from the mirror and circled his arm

around her shoulder, his face close. "You're still beautiful to me and to the friends waiting just beyond this door." He waved toward the hallway. "And given a chance, you'd be surprised how loving these Christians can be. You're never alone in a group like this, or with me—especially with me." Lauren felt herself relax into his arms. "I don't want you to leave, Lauren. I need you as much as you need me."

The crushing weight of decision forced its way once again upon her moment of pleasure, smothering any embers of happiness like a drizzling rain. "It's not that easy, Jason."

Jason studied her for a long moment before dropping a kiss on her forehead. "I know." He loosened his embrace and prodded her toward the hallway. "But if you're like me, things are always clearer on a full stomach."

The next hour sped by as Lauren visited with her guests and listened to those eager to catch her up with island news. She finally emptied her plate, awkward as that was left-handed, and laid it aside. Tasting everything at the insistence of others nearly put her stomach over the top. She leaned back into the sofa, noticing for the first time an aching sensation from her right arm. She had no idea where Jason had placed the medicine or the instruction sheet. Certainly one of the pain pills was due. She looked across the room were Jason was busy showering praise on the ladies for their fine cooking.

"Tilly, you've outdone yourself," he exclaimed, taking a huge bite from a slice of Stollen bread.

Tilly blushed and waved him off. "Wait until Lauren gets the recipe. She'll make it even better than me. You wait and see!"

Both glanced her direction, and Lauren rolled her eyes. Jason chuckled, pausing long enough to send her a wink before moving on to talk with the two men examining the repaired door. The medication could wait, she finally determined, finding no appropriate opportunity to disentangle herself from the ladies who kept her occupied in conversation. A few minutes later, Tilly began covering the food dishes with foil.

"It's time to let the girl have her rest," Tilly announced to the group. "Did someone bring more foil?"

The women slowly separated and began the massive job of cleanup, refusing Lauren's offer of help. She watched silently as dish after dish made its way to the kitchen. Tilly placed a full plate of chocolate brownies on the counter, sealing the foil edges as she slid it into the corner. She took a final look about, obviously pleased with the results, and made her way to the sofa where Lauren sat.

"Finally a second or two to talk without interruption," Tilly replied, dropping herself into the sofa. The cushion sandwiched her hips in a deep vee. "Because I have something to tell ya."

The seriousness of her tone gained Lauren's interest. "Is something wrong?"

"Don't know," Tilly answered strangely. "You had a call this morning from that boyfriend of yours in Cincinnati."

"Tom?" Lauren groaned. "When did he call?" She didn't wait for the answer as words spilled over each other in horror. "You didn't tell him out about the break-in, did you?"

"Yes." Tilly gave the word a curious stress that sounded affronted. "He asked where you were and what was goin' on. Couldn't lie to him." She used the corner of her apron to wipe a smear of chocolate off her hand.

"What did he say?"

"Nothin' much," she answered in a decidedly strained voice. "Said he'd call tonight. Guess he'd finished whatever testing he had to take."

"That all?" Suspicion pointed to more.

"Well," Tilly hedged.

"Yes?"

"He did ask about the ferry schedule."

"What!" Lauren lowered her voice when Jason shot her a quick look from across the room. "I can't have Tom coming here. Jason's threatening to camp out on the deck tonight." Her mind whirled desperately. "Did Tom say when he was coming?"

"No," Tilly answered. "He didn't say he was coming at all. He just asked about the ferry schedule, that's all." She patted Lauren's knee. "He said he'd call tonight. I'm assumin' he meant from Cincinnati."

Lauren calmed. "You're right! He'll probably call tonight and try to convince me he should come." She bit her lip in contemplation. "He wouldn't just come." *I hope.*

"See! Nothin' to worry about." Tilly lumbered up and out of the sofa. She looked over at Jason, who was still talking with the men. "I'm glad he's stayin' out here tonight. Makes me feel a boatload better. But you're gonna spend the night at my place."

Lauren opened her mouth to protest but Tilly cut her off. "You and Jason don't need to set tongues wagging all over again. Now, let me shoo these folks outta here so you can get some rest, and I can go make up my guest bed for you."

Jason turned and gave Tilly a knowing smile as if he'd heard. Lauren ran her fingers nervously through her hair, feeling its disheveled condition. She couldn't wait until everyone left so she could take a much needed shower.

❧

"You can't take a shower with the cast," Jason pointed out logically, pulling back the plastic curtain. "The showerhead's up too high. You'll get everything wet."

"What about using plastic wrap around the cast?" Lauren asked. A good, hot shower was all she really wanted, a daily function she'd taken for granted—until today. Was it too much to hope for now?

Jason only shook his head. "True, wrapping the arm might keep it dry, but just the same you shouldn't try showering until you're no longer woozy." He studied the fixtures. "What's wrong with a bath?"

"I'd never be able wash my hair without breaking my neck," she pointed out. The cast was proving to be more of a complication than she expected. "Maybe if I did my hair first, before the bath, I could lean under the spigot."

"Maybe." He gave a thoughtful glance at the tub. "With the cast on your right arm and spigot on this end, you'll have more than your share of difficulty." His eyes roamed the room. "Well, there's only one thing to do."

"What?" She didn't like the determined look on his face.

He reached over her head for two towels on the rack above the commode. "I'll have to wash your hair for you."

Lauren stepped back. "You can't do that!" she sputtered. "It's not—not appropriate."

"Don't be a prude," he said, ignoring her objections as he draped one towel over her shoulders. "Now, find a comfortable place to lean over the tub edge so I can get the water going." Placing the other towel across the cold porcelain, he moved to her other side.

"Jason Levitte, this is ridiculous," she voiced, clumsily finding her way to the floor. "What will the neighbors say?"

He chuckled, turning the faucet handles. "You worry too much about the neighbors. They're not in here."

"It's not funny."

His smile said otherwise. "There's absolutely nothing wrong with me washing your hair. Male hairstylists do it all the time."

"At the salon, maybe, but not in a woman's cramped bathroom."

"Location, location, location—is that it?" His hand tested the water. "Perfect!" He turned suddenly and left the bathroom.

"Jason!"

Before she could get to her feet again, he returned, brandishing a large pitcher. "Try to turn this way," he said, guiding her cast to rest on the towel. "Lean your head down over the tub. That's it."

He filled the pitcher, and Lauren felt the rush of warm water stream across the back of her neck then pour over her forehead. Jason's hand gently tilted her head to each side, moving her hair until it became thoroughly wet.

"Pull back a little," he instructed, and Lauren heard the

familiar wheeze of shampoo being expressed from the bottle. A flowery smell filled the room. "Back a little more."

Lauren did as commanded, her eyes tightly closed. The situation bordered on crazy, but no argument could change Jason's mind once set. How well she knew that!

"I've never seen sparkly blue shampoo before," he said, massaging the suds into her scalp.

"That's because it's a girl thing." She began to relax under the caring, soothing touch of his hands. If she were totally honest with herself, she'd admit how good it felt to be cared for by Jason—even if the pressure of leaning over the bathtub did threaten to explode her head.

"Time to rinse," he announced, smoothly steering her head farther over the tub edge. Once again he repeated the shampooing process, this time in silence. Suddenly he stopped.

"What's wrong?" she questioned, tasting a bitter bubble of soap. His continued silence caused her to turn slightly, eyes still tightly closed. "What is it, Jason?"

Unhurriedly, his fingers began to work again. "I was just thinking about the past."

*Could that be good?* Lauren waited in silence.

"Your hair has always been stunning, Lauren," he continued. "Even short, it's beautiful." All movement stopped for a second time. "I just hope you didn't cut it because of me."

Her long tresses had been his pride and joy. She couldn't help but remember the bolt of revenge each snip embedded in her heart and mind as lock after lock fell soundlessly to the tile floor. But the act never did rid her of his memory. Like her hair which sold for wigs, the memory of his love stayed alive and circulating somewhere unknown.

Lauren tilted back trying to catch a glimpse of Jason through watery eyes. Why didn't he speak? But his blurry image quickly faded into nothing as a burning sensation forced her to duck back under the water. "The soap's in my eyes!"

"Wait a minute," he commanded, quickly rinsing her hair with one hand and wiping her eyes with the other. "Here, use the towel." He drew her back from the water, helping her upright.

Lauren felt a soft towel press into her open hand, and she quickly dabbed her eyes as Jason began using the other to soak up the streams of water spilling from her hair.

Abruptly he stopped.

Water dripped on her leg. What now! Blinking rapidly, she turned, glimpsing the source of Jason's silence.

There in the doorway stood Tom Thurman.

# *fifteen*

"Tom!" Lauren could only stare wide-eyed at the tall figure filling the small doorway.

He was dressed in dark blue shorts and a T-shirt, and Tom's black hair seemed naturally outfitted to the ensemble, harmonizing to fit his usually unpretentious character. Right now, however, his low-lidded gaze was anything but harmonious.

Strained silence hung in the air like morning fog—cold and clammy.

Jason was the first to recover. "You must be Tom Thurman," he greeted, wiping one wet hand across his jeans before extending it.

"And you must be Jason Levitte," Tom replied in a carefully modulated voice, slowly accepting his hand. His gaze lit expectantly on Lauren.

Trepidation suddenly made it hard to breathe. "Why, Tom, I wasn't expecting you."

"That much is obvious," he said dryly.

Lauren was definitely at a disadvantage, crouched uncomfortably on the cold tile floor, water dripping off her nose like a small child. *Why, oh why, can't my life be normal like most folks?* Using the edge of the towel, she quickly dabbed the offending drops. "As you can see, I'm in the process of getting my hair washed," she explained, moving the cast into better view, "and Jason is helping with this seemingly impossible task." She cast a meaningful look at Tom, then Jason. "And I'm finding this situation extremely awkward at the moment. Would you gentlemen mind very much excusing me to finish?"

Tom said nothing, but stared between the two as he gradually backed out of the room and walked down the hallway.

Jason stood, offering a hand to hoist her up. "I'll talk to him."

"You will do no such thing!" she responded breathlessly, capturing his arm in a tight grip. "That's the last thing I need." A sudden wave of dizziness overtook her, and she stumbled backward.

Jason quickly steadied her. "The first thing you need to do is get some sleep."

"Stood up too quickly, that's all," she excused, moving from his hold. "Maybe it'd be best if you went home until I've had a chance to talk to him."

"Absolutely not!" He planted both hands on her shoulders, turning her squarely in front of him, and gave her a look of determination she knew all too well. "You're going to haul yourself into the bedroom and get some shut-eye." He cut off all protest. "You're in no condition to deal with anything, much less ex-boyfriends," he added with a whisper. Before she could object to his erroneous conclusion concerning Tom, he prodded her out the door, across the hall, and through her bedroom doorway. "Don't let me see you for at least four hours."

He quickly crossed the hall again, then returned with her pain pills and a plastic cup filled with water. "Open wide," he teased, holding a pain pill in front of her face.

"But I haven't even taken my bath—"

"Later!"

She took the pill from his hand and set it on her tongue, then took several sips of the cool water before handing the cup back to Jason. She tried to protest again. "But—"

"No buts!" he whispered, softly closing the door behind him until it clicked.

Lauren looked about the room, anger welling like spring as she flung the wet towel from her neck and onto the wicker chair. Of all the nerve! She ripped the bedcovers back. Just what she needed; Jason and Tom holed up in the living room having a tête-à-tête. And Jason thought she could sleep through that. "Ha!" The bitter laugh was nothing more than a chirp.

The bed groaned under her brusque flop, the pillows receiving much the same as she punched them to shape with both hands. Instantly she wished she hadn't as throbs of pain echoed through the broken arm in protest. Fortunately, a few moments of stillness encouraged the pain to subside.

Lauren hadn't expected to sleep, but physical weariness finally overcame her tumultuous and confused emotional state. She awoke to find the late afternoon sun pouring through the open curtains of the back window. Groaning, she turned onto her side stretching to see the bedside clock. Five-thirty! It'd been less than two hours, and she didn't feel particularly refreshed, a leftover drug haze still plaguing her body. Wearily she flopped to her back, staring at the ceiling, listening for any telltale signs of Jason or Tom. Hearing none, she gradually sat up, willing full wakefulness upon herself.

From the edge of the bed, the wall mirror took in her scruffy appearance, and she moaned. The wet, stringy hair had dried into nothing short of a frizzy bird's nest with unruly tangles.

"Same to you," she mumbled at the offending reflection as she padded over to the bureau to grab the wooden-handle brush.

Clumsily she brushed with her left hand, tearing at the roots as bristles caught every unseen knot. Finally, several strokes later, her hair turned almost manageable. She smoothed out her wrinkled shorts outfit before carefully opening the bedroom door. Cautiously, she peered into the empty hallway. All was quiet. She ventured toward the living room.

Rhythmic ticking from the rooster clock mounted above the fireplace reverberated loudly in the silence. The front door stood open, and Lauren quietly peeked through the screen, discovering Tom asleep in the Adirondack chair, his leather sandals propped on the picnic table. Jason was still nowhere to be seen. Noiselessly she backed from the door and made her way to the bathroom. Finally, the bath she desperately needed. . . Tom could wait. And what Jason didn't know wouldn't hurt him.

Lauren found the hot, scented bubble bath dissolved much of the weariness from her limbs and gave her time to think. Surprise would have been too mild a term to express her reaction to Tom's arrival. Beyond her own worries, she hoped Tom hadn't risked his pastoral exams by coming to the island. He'd no doubt come to her aid with heroic measures in mind, a knight making a chivalrous rescue for his damsel in distress, only to find another man wearing his suit of armor. What a disastrous turn of events, poor timing, and a terrible misconstruing of the facts.

What could she say to Tom? He'd sent her to Bay Island in an effort to save their relationship, an opportunity to get things right with God. Now she had nothing to offer. Nothing! She didn't love him. The first seeds of doubt, planted well before her arrival to Bay Island, had grown into full realization. Even their friendship would suffer inevitable demise when she explained this newfound insight toward their ill-fated romance, when he learned she didn't love him like a woman should. He'd never settle for the brother-sister routine. Even the fact she'd made no commitment whatsoever to Jason would be of little consolation for this ultimate blow. She dreaded the moment of disclosure which was close upon her.

And Jason? Where did he come off assuming Tom and she were through? Never once had she indicated it to be so. She'd never given answer to his summer request or discussed any real future plans.

A light knock at the door startled Lauren. "Yes?"

"Are you okay in there?" Tom called softly.

"Yes," she repeated, her former nervousness returning. "I'm nearly finished."

"Just be careful." He paused, then asked, "Do you need any help?"

"No. I'm just fine."

"That's good." He sounded relieved.

"Are you alone?" she ventured to ask, repositioning the cast on the tub's edge.

"Yes. Your—friend left awhile ago, but said he'd return this evening."

Lauren thought a moment. "I won't be long. If you're hungry, there's plenty in the refrigerator. Just help yourself."

"Do you want me to fix you something?"

"No." She still felt stuffed, no better than a fat Thanksgiving turkey. "But you get whatever you want. I promise not to be long."

A second later she heard him retreat back up the hallway. Quickly she rinsed, stepped from the tub, and grabbed a towel to dry, finding even this effort a most difficult one. She gave an elaborate sigh as the robe sash finally tightened, and she hurriedly glanced out the door before making a mad dash to the bedroom.

Trying to clear one leg at a time into her plaid shorts turned into a major event. Twice she practically tumbled as her toes snagged the waistband first and then the hem. Finally she completed dressing, frustrated, but presentable.

Tom stood at the kitchen counter replacing the foil top on a casserole dish. Immediately he looked her way, his watchful and wary consideration evident. "Feeling better?" he asked, crimping the shiny foil securely over the edges.

"Much better." She sensed his apprehension matched her own. "Did you find enough to eat?"

He nodded, gesturing to the casserole dish. "Are you sure you don't want something? I can heat up another square of lasagna."

"No thanks," she answered, wondering just how they were to get beyond the niceties. Hesitantly she extended her good hand toward him. "Can we talk?"

He took this encouraging sign and made his way to her side, grasping her hand in his own. "I'm sorry for being such a cad when I arrived," he apologized straight away. "I was awfully worried after hearing you were robbed and went to the hospital." A slight smile touched his mouth. "I don't know what I expected to find when I got here, but it wasn't the sight of you sitting on the bathroom floor having a daily beauty treatment—or answering questions about your well-being to some guy on the phone."

Lauren gave a puzzled look. "Some guy?"

"Larry somebody. He called while you were asleep."

"Ah," she acknowledged, leading Tom outside to the shaded picnic table. "That would be the police officer who was here last night." It seemed best to keep things simple. Unimportant facts would only complicate matters.

Tom shrugged as he sat next to her. "I don't think he said."

There was an aching pause.

"Tom?"

"Uh-oh," he murmured, taking a deep breath. "Here it comes."

"Please don't say that," she pleaded, squeezing his hand. The situation was difficult enough without seeing the dejected expression crossing his handsome face. "First I need to know how your exams went. You didn't jeopardize them by coming to the island, did you?"

"No," he answered quickly enough. "The last exam finished late yesterday, and I'm sure I did well."

"You didn't get scores yet?"

"Post-examine interviews and scores were this afternoon. Those I missed."

Lauren digested this for a moment. "I hope it won't look poorly for you. I'd hate to be the cause—"

Tom turned toward her, closing what little gap existed between them. "It wouldn't have mattered, Lauren. With the exception of God, you've always been first, and I couldn't have stayed in Cincinnati, not knowing you were hurt and at the hospital. There wasn't even a question about my coming."

"You're one of the sweetest people I know," she said sadly, caressing his cheek as she stood. "That's what makes this so much harder for me to say."

"This is where the uh-oh part comes in." He paused, eyeing her, then held out his hand again. "Come on and sit down. Whatever you have to say will be easier sitting down."

She looked at him steadily, finally taking his hand before she sat down. Tom had always been of a gentle nature, compassionate and understanding when the walls of trouble closed in about her. His rock-strong approach had steadied her more than once. He wasn't headstrong and absorbed with life like Jason or impulsive as Larry, just firm and solid. A girl couldn't hope for more. So why did her feelings of love fizzle like a wet firecracker with the man? She knew the answer might elude her for life, but the recognizable truth it produced could not be ignored or pushed aside.

Gathering courage, she met his gaze straight on. "Tom, you sent me to the island hoping I'd find the path to God, to serve Him fully again. I think that's happening." Abruptly she stood again, finding the need to pace and maintain space between them. She moved behind a lawn chair, one hand braced on the frame. "The first thing I've discovered is the beginnings of forgiveness. What I'd called forgiveness before wasn't forgiveness at all. There's a big difference between real forgiveness and the ability to file away the problem and the feelings associated with it. When I came back to the island last weekend, the file came back out, the very same file I'd stashed away five years ago, and it was still stuffed with every hurtful memory and allegation."

Tom leaned forward listening intently.

"I'm still learning the essence of this forgiveness, but I believe God is finally getting the message through this thick skull of mine." She tapped her temple for emphasis. "The second thing I discovered is that God isn't calling me to foreign missions." She waited for a reaction.

His unreadable face told her nothing. "Go on."

"In that same light," she continued, "I've also discovered I'm unworthy of your love and devotion." She met his blank stare. "Although I love you dearly, it's not the type of love you ought to have from a future wife." Suddenly she moved to his side. "It wasn't supposed to turn out like this—it just did."

"Poor Lauren." Tom touched her hair lightly for a moment. "I can't say I'm happy to hear the news, but I've suspected for quite awhile."

"You knew!"

"I knew something wasn't right," he answered. "I didn't know if the problem rested in your relationship with God, with me, or both."

Lauren drew a weary breath. "But now it's gone sour, hasn't it—for both of us?"

"It's never sour when God makes the plans," Tom reminded. "This wasn't perhaps what I'd originally intended when you came to the island, but. . ." He seemed momentarily without words. "And Jason? Are you still in love with him?"

Lauren colored. "Yes," she said after a momentary hesitation. She shifted uncomfortably under his penetrating stare. "But there are still unresolved issues, and I'm not sure what hope, if any, exists." She spread out her left hand helplessly. "I haven't a clue what to do. Jason's asked me to stay the summer, to give it a chance, to see what might happen."

"What did you tell him?"

"Nothing."

"Nothing?"

"I'm not sure what I should do," Lauren said miserably. "There's my job and apartment to consider."

"Have you prayed?"

"A lot!" She sighed. "Sometimes I just wish God made phone calls, especially when there seems to be no answer to the question."

"He does answer," Tom remarked in all seriousness. "He just doesn't use the phone."

"What?"

"Take time to mediate on His Word, and He'll speak to you."

That she knew. "Tom?"

"Hmm?"

"You need to know my feelings for Jason in no way affected my decision about our relationship."

"I know." Warmly he took her outstretched hands. "And Jason's head over heels in love with you. You know that, don't you?"

"What's makes you say such a thing?" she asked, puzzled, her voice giving a slight betraying quiver.

"We talked a little bit."

She frowned, her brow pinched. This couldn't be good.

"Don't worry." He laughed. "He didn't reveal any deep, dark secrets. It was his demeanor, his actions which told me. He's very protective of you. I'd only hoped my initial impressions were wrong, but his asking you to stay the summer confirms the notion." His smile waned. "And I give you my blessing, whatever you choose."

Lauren blinked. She was frankly taken aback by his calm acceptance. Not that she wanted him heartbroken, but there should have been some reaction. "What will you do?"

"Go to the mission field as planned," he announced with certainty. "Now that I know how things stand at home, I'll move forward with those plans."

"I feel terribly miserable about this, Tom."

"Don't!" He gently rubbed her back as he'd done so many times. "Be thankful God's given us the answer. Trusting God means trusting His answers whether we like them or not."

Lauren gave an understanding nod. Tom was right. He'd always grasped the intended spiritual parallel of life's situations, the parallels she so often missed. "What are you going to do right now?"

"Well," he began, "that funny friend of yours, Tilly, offered me a place to stay tonight. She said one of the nearby cabins is vacant this week."

"Tilly? You met her?"

"You've had one busy afternoon while you napped. Tilly came visiting with another woman not long after Jason left."

"Oh!"

"Anyway, she's going to show me to the cabin as soon as Jason gets back, and I'll go home in the morning." Both looked up as a large black car came up the road slowly approaching the incline. "And it looks like my relief is here."

# sixteen

"A bit of fresh air will do you good," Jason told Lauren as he wheeled her open golf cart onto the main road. "It'll help clear out the cobwebs."

Lauren was busy looking at the lakeshore. "I suppose." The episode with Tom had left her completely exhausted and relieved at the same time. In retrospect, the separation gave her freedom, some open space to grow—and the feeling of sadness. The fact her life must irrevocably change seemed more than a little unsettling. A small part of her wanted to cling to her old life like a suction cup clings to the window, gradually loosening, gradually breaking the seal with dryness until the complete detachment is ready and expected.

She remembered similar feelings while attending camp during her eleventh year. The exciting week of new friends and new bonds came to an end way too soon. For the first time, she'd felt the emotional pull between the old and the new, between the home she knew and the world she'd discovered. She'd learned how impossible it was to maintain both without taking in one area in order to give in another.

This juncture had presented itself again. She'd released Tom to follow the path set before him, forcing her to find a path of her own. But her own passageway was fraught with options and less than concrete facts with which to make wise choices.

"Hey, there!"

Lauren looked up, startled at Jason's laughter.

"I'd thought you'd dozed off there for a minute." His disarming smile nearly took her breath away. "Not very good for my ego, you know."

Lauren laughed with him. "Sorry!"

"I think you'll find the spot up ahead will do wonders for your wandering mind." Jason made a narrow turn onto a graveled back road. "Besides pizza, I know your other vices, cookies and cream being one of them." Amusement crept into his voice. "I believe you mentioned ice cream earlier this morning."

The man wasn't about to let her forget the state he'd found her in that morning, Lauren thought with chagrin. What Jason found to be endearing, she found most awkward. Never in her life had she felt so euphorically out of control as she had during that time.

"Here we are!" Jason announced, steering the cart to a stop between freshly painted yellow lines of the half-full parking lot.

To her horror, she immediately recognized the Dairy Barn. Visions of Mr. Edwards filled her head. The event seemed miles away in time, but in fact, it'd only been last night since the obligatory ice-cream cone ordeal.

"Surprised?" he asked, obviously misinterpreting her expression for one of pleasure. "It's much bigger and nicer than the building they had at their old site. I think the new look and location's been good for business." He quickly slipped out his side and circled to her. "Come on." His hand extended to hers.

Lauren hesitated only a moment before accepting his grasp. She couldn't very well refuse to go in. What would she say? No, she could only hope the old man wasn't working tonight. With her hand still firmly in Jason's hold, she followed him through the double set of clear, heavy doors. The sight of Mr. Edwards' gray head and slim figure behind the counter quickly dashed her hopes.

"Hello, Van," Jason called in greeting as they neared the ice-cream case. "You remember Lauren!"

The owlish face turned her way, eyes narrowed in deliberation behind the thick glasses. "Yep, I remember." He finished giving change to another customer before his glance lit on her again, focusing on the sling first and then her face.

"Hello, Mr. Edwards," Lauren returned clumsily.

Jason gave her a smile. "I bet you didn't know Van now owns the Dairy Barn." He turned to Mr. Edwards, his smile never wavering. "What do you recommend this evening?"

Mr. Edwards used a thumb to push his glasses up a notch on his bulbous nose. A moment of hesitation followed before he spoke. "Might I recommend the flavor of the week: cookies and cream?"

Lauren thought she'd drop straight through the floor into the basement.

Jason seemed oblivious to the tension and gladly ordered. "Make it two in waffle cones." He pulled money from his wallet.

The old man slowly slid the curved, glass cover back and reached deep into the crevasse with a wet, silver scoop while she looked on. Jason had called him by his first name. Van! Lauren couldn't ever remember hearing the man referred to as anything but Mr. Edwards. She wasn't even sure until this very moment he had a first name. Certainly there were people who knew him on a first-name basis, but his gruff exterior kept most at bay—everyone except Jason, that is. Leave it to Jason to break through.

Mr. Edwards handed one filled waffle cone to Jason who in turn passed it to Lauren. Gingerly, she accepted the cold treat and waited patiently as the old man began filling the second cone. Silently, she looked about, watching the many people who sat at the parlor-style tables. Jason had been right. The place did look clean and bright, evidently thriving under new management. But where were the workers? Thinking back, she couldn't recall any staff on duty the night before, either. Surely he didn't run the place by himself.

"There you go, young man," Mr. Edwards said, handing Jason the second cone.

Jason thanked the old man as he made change from the cash register and dropped the clinking coins noisily into his pocket.

"Let's go to the tables outside," Jason suggested, snatching several napkins as he passed the condiment table. He opened the door for her.

Lauren followed him to the farthest concrete picnic table under a large oak. Nestled next to a man-made pond, she watched two ducks clamber out of the water toward them in hopes of a handout. A warm breeze rustled the leaves, and she took in the sweet air.

"I think you're right," Lauren began. "This property is so much nicer than their old place. It's so picturesque and quiet."

Jason nodded. "The Dairy Barn was given a fair price for their land, and the option to set up at Levitte's Landing or here. When management saw this piece of land, they took it right away. After a year, though, they sold the business. I'm not sure how or why Mr. Edwards acquired it. It was a closed-door deal."

"He seems a little bit over his head trying to work the counter and the tables. I noticed he doesn't have much help." A drip of ice cream plopped onto her shorts.

Jason dabbed the spot away. "He can't keep his staff." He threw her a mischievous smile. "Some think he's a little rough around the edges. Imagine that!"

"Really?" Lauren laughed with mock surprise.

They lapsed into a companionable silence. One duck ventured close enough, and Jason broke a piece from his cone to toss at the waiting mallard. Lauren's thoughts returned to Tilly's advice. *It's time to stop being so self-absorbed. Jason is a businessman. He shoulders a lot of responsibility trying to keep his company profitable. A good woman could help him, side up with him—join him. Do you know what Jason's dreams might be?*

"Jason?"

"Hmm?" He tossed another crumb at the lingering bird and turned toward her.

"Have you ever thought about where you want to be in ten years?"

His eyebrows inched up with uncertainty. "You mean with the business?"

Lauren shrugged. "Not necessarily." Two more ducks began to congregate at their feet, and she tossed the remaining remnant of her cone toward them. "Certainly your business plays an important part in who you are and what you want, but there must be other dreams apart from your work."

"Like what?"

"You know! Dreams like. . ." She waved her hand about as if trying to pluck words out of the air. "Like being cast for the lead role in the summer theatre production of *Fiddler on the Roof,* or maybe taking a white-water rafting trip."

"Well," he hesitated, a smile tugging at the corners of his mouth, "I can safely say I've never had the urge to be an actor or to risk life and limb on an oversized rubber raft."

Lauren took a steadying breath. "Then what would you like do if time and money were no object?"

"You really want to know?" He seemed cautiously surprised, abandoning his former teasing mood.

"Yes."

"First and foremost, I always want to be in God's will no matter where I am or what I do," he answered in all seriousness. "And one of these days I'd like to take a more active role at church, maybe the office of church deacon or trustee. They never seem to have enough men willing to run for either office."

"You'd make a good deacon," Lauren commented, knowing how needed and beneficial a compassionate spirit would be in that position. "I'm surprised they haven't asked you."

Lauren abruptly hurried him along. "What else? What other things would you like to accomplish?"

He laughed, his eyes twinkling impishly. "Well. . . ," he hesitated, rubbing his hand across his chin in thought, "there are several places I'd like to visit around the country. I always thought it'd be interesting to go across the country by train or maybe take a steamer excursion trip." A wistful look crossed his face.

Jason never expressed an interest in trains before. Had she been too self-absorbed to bother with his ideas as Tilly suggested? "I didn't know you liked trains."

"Been hooked on them since I was five and got my first electric train." He laughed, obviously finding the memory a happy one. "I have several boxes of those trains packed away in the attic and one of these days. . ." He paused, his expression pensive. "One of these days, I'm going to set up every one of those trains in the living room like we used to at Christmas. I might even try my hand at garden railroading." His smile widened. "All I need is a garden."

Her own words came back. *I wouldn't mind having a house with enough land for a little garden. Maybe some tomatoes, corn, peppers. . .and some lettuce. And while I'm dreaming, one of those easy garden tillers would be nice.* "Those are nice dreams, Jason."

Jason leaned toward her, his head tilted quizzically as he released the crumpled napkins he held on to the table. Gently, he took her hand. "What's this all about?" His voice, like his touch, was a caress.

He smiled down at her so tenderly, she lowered her gaze. "I'm just realizing how very little I really know about you." This insight accompanied another revelation; she wanted to know everything there was to know about the man beside her.

"Don't you know you're the only person who really does know me?" He met her stunned amazement with a hint of laughter in his eyes. "It's true. You know how I think and operate. You already know how bullheaded I can be."

Yes, that she did know. Firsthand! Yet, she didn't know what made him tick on the inside, outside his business dealings. Could it have been because the business commanded his every minute during those early years, or because she couldn't see past the demanding force his business implied? Or a combination of both? She'd loved him beyond what she thought capable back then, never once dreaming anything could pull them apart—even the business. Then the unthinkable happened, destroying everything in its path, a mudslide of turmoil and hurt washing an entire five years away.

And she still loved Jason. Just one tender look from his gray eyes or the touch of his hand melted her insides to jelly. Even now, her heart ached to be held by him, to feel his breath on her hair. Yet she couldn't rely on her emotions! Jason had yet to explain why he built her house or what role, if any, Becky Merrill played in his life. Either of the two could easily change their future course of events.

"Lauren!" She looked up at his teasing eyes, laughter lurking in their depths. "Do you know just how beautiful you are when you're thinking too hard?" Gently he drew her head against his shoulder, lowering his clean-shaven cheek against hers. "Tell me you'll stay the summer," he murmured.

Lauren basked in the moment, nearly throwing all caution to the wind as she looked up. He lifted her chin gently and, lowering his head, placed his lips tenderly on her own.

"Jason," she responded breathlessly. "I—"

The moment burst quicker than a pricked balloon when his cell phone rang. Both stiffened and remained still. He made no immediate move to answer it, but the interruption had already caused the damage, breaking the mood—and her spirits. The phone persisted, and Lauren slowly moved from his embrace. She heard Jason sigh as he reached for the phone clipped to his belt.

"Yes," he answered brusquely into the phone, annoyance coating the edge of his voice. He remained silent a moment as he listened, turning slightly from Lauren before he stood.

Lauren sensed his want of privacy and swiveled to face the other direction. Yet his low voice carried.

"Now, Bec, this is something Anderson could have handled." His voice lowered another degree, now barely audible. "I'm with a client. . ."

The remaining words drifted off into oblivion as he reached the bank of the pond. Client! He'd told the caller she was a client. No doubt the caller, Bec, was none other than Becky Merrill. Lauren's hands trembled, and her stomach tightened. Not once, but twice, he'd told the beautiful woman a lie concerning her. The deceit could have only one purpose, a means to keep both women in the dark. Still she was hesitant to believe it. Jason wasn't perfect, but he'd never intentionally hurt anyone.

But she'd heard the incriminating words from his own lips, the very same lips that had but a moment ago sealed their kiss. Her mind reeled with possibilities. Maybe he'd committed himself to the other woman, never dreaming Lauren would ever return to the island, and suddenly found himself in a tight spot. But how long did he think the charade could continue if she stayed the summer? Panic filled her as she realized just how close she'd come to agreeing.

Hurt threatened to explode her heart.

Giving a hard stare at his turned back, Lauren stood with as much dignity as she could muster and brushed the fine dust of crumbs from her lap. At least she didn't have stay here and watch. Marching off to the golf cart, she plopped hard into the passenger seat, cupping her sling for support. If she had any courage, she'd leave him to walk home.

But she didn't have to wait long.

"I'm sorry for the interruption, Lauren," he apologized the moment he rounded the cart and sat behind the wheel. "I told her not to call me unless it was an emergency." He still sounded annoyed.

"Maybe she didn't think your client was important enough to hold your calls for," Lauren retorted, anger quickly displacing the hurt.

Two perplexed lines appeared between his straight blond brows. "What's that supposed to mean?"

"It means your appointment is over, and I'd like to be taken home." Lauren didn't dare look at Jason, but stared straight ahead into the ice-cream shop's window. Absently wiping tables and peering at them with interest was Mr. Edwards. She knew Jason saw the old man's curious attention.

"Just what I need," he muttered, turning the ignition, "an audience." His arm brushed against her as he backed the cart up. "And as for you, my girl, when we reach Piney Point, you're going to explain to me exactly what your problem is."

"I'll be happy to," she flung back at him. "I'll make everything wonderfully clear, because when I leave Bay Island this time, it'll be for good."

# seventeen

The ride to the cottage grew stiff with tension as dusk fell. Brief but frequent glances from Jason told her his anger simmered close to the top. It was there in the thinness of his lips and the jutting of his jaw, yet he seemed to be exercising great self-restraint and remained silent. Lauren said not a word, her mind whirling ahead to the unavoidable collision due between Jason and herself. Fingering the sling's soft material, she fixed her eyes demurely ahead to the road. It wasn't until they reached Piney Point, and he quietly and firmly snapped off the ignition, that either spoke. Lauren assumed she'd go first, but Jason snatched the ball in play, his offense strategy ready to take the field.

"Lauren, I don't know what it is you want from me," he began, sounding exasperated as he turned toward her, his eyes probing her face. "Do you want me to quit the business, to sell it off? Is that what you want? Would that finally make you happy?"

"Absolutely not!" Lauren retorted, slightly puzzled. It seemed apparent Jason had erroneously assumed the source of her unhappiness lay with his business. "What makes you think your business has anything to do with this?"

"You've never hidden the fact how much you detest the demands the business places on my time." He gave her a hard stare and continued. "But I thought you understood the reasons for my departure the other day. I had no other choice, you knew that. What would you have had me do?" Lauren would have gladly answered, but he didn't give her a chance. "There will always be times when a phone call needs to be answered or instances when I'm called away or our time together might be interrupted or cut short. That's part of the territory, Lauren." He took a deep breath as if readying himself to wind another pitch. "I've done everything I could to bend over backward this week to spend time with you, including the delegation of my work to other associates. The demands aren't as great as they were years ago, but there are responsibilities that still require my attention. I don't see why you can't accept that."

She took advantage of a slight pause. "I understand the demands of your job perfectly," she told him firmly. "I may not like them, but I understand them." Not once had she voiced a disparaging remark to him about the business since arriving on the island, and his callous acceptance of these accusations hurt deeply. What kind of woman did he take her for? "Your business responsibilities are not the problem."

Jason drew an impatient breath. "Then would you kindly tell me what is?"

"It's about trust and respect, Jason." She raised her chin militantly. "I don't like being referred to as a client or an appointment so you can—can schmooze it up with your secretary."

"What!" His voice boomed in disbelief as he stared at her in amazement.

Lauren raised appealing eyes to heaven. The man was going to deny it. "Was the phone call tonight from your secretary, Becky Merrill?"

He paused briefly before answering. "Yes!" Then more slowly, "Why?"

"When she called, you told her you were with a client." She waved off the protest she saw brewing, her voice calm, but icy. "I had to ask myself why you would do such a thing." She now waved her hand carelessly in the air. "I might not have thought anything of it, except for the phone call your secretary made to me the morning you left the island for South Carolina. At that time, I was your appointment!" Disgust overtook her voice. "She asked me to reschedule our meeting time. Granted, you might not consider fixing my roof a date, but it certainly wasn't an appointment."

He looked puzzled. "Lauren, I haven't a clue what you're talking about."

"Are you denying the fact you told Becky Merrill, just minutes ago, I was your client?"

His surprise seemed genuine, but Lauren refused to be moved.

"Yes, I'm denying it!" His gray eyes narrowed in thought. "I'm trying my best to think back to exactly what I did say." He rubbed the back of his neck, a motion Lauren found oddly defenseless.

But she didn't let up. "And did you lead your secretary to believe I was your appointment the morning you were called away?"

"Definitely not!" Something in his defensive tone spoke of momentary bewilderment. "Why would I have done either? It just doesn't make sense."

Lauren swung herself from the cart. "Five years is a long time. It wouldn't be so unexpected to find you might be—be committed to someone else. But I don't expect you to lead me on in one direction when you're not free to do so—deceiving some other poor girl in the process. It's unconscionable."

"Let's stick to one accusation at a time, shall we?" he flung back, his face grim. "You're flying all over the place. How's a person expected to defend himself when you keep changing the charges?"

Lauren didn't move, her cheeks flushed with indignation. How could Jason try to skirt the real issue when faced with the truth? "How indeed!" In anger, she marched to the steps.

But Jason raced ahead, barring her way, frowning heavily. For several palpable moments they squared off glances.

"There must be some explanation, and we're not going anywhere until we discover exactly what that explanation is." A muscle moved at the side of his mouth as he silently appraised her, and she guessed the inward struggle he was having to get himself under control. "Frankly, I'm getting a little tired of these misunderstandings."

"Well, if there's an explanation, I'll be glad to hear it," Lauren responded in an expressionless tone. There could be no possible explanation, no matter how much she longed to think there might be.

"Sit down a minute and let me think," he demanded, rubbing his neck again.

Lauren sank willingly onto the wooden step and waited. "I'm listening."

In the waning light, his face bore a haggard look, and Lauren felt her heart lurch. Instantly, her mind returned to another time, a time when the tables were turned. She was the accused and he the accuser. Persuasive proof convicted her then, even as later evidence proved it wrong. Could she have misjudged this situation in much the same way?

"You say Becky asked you to reschedule our appointment the morning I left?" he asked, and Lauren nodded. "I suppose that doesn't surprise me since Becky knows nothing of our relationship."

Lauren winced. "I see." A chilling sensation coursed through her at the thought of Jason and Becky together.

"You're jumping to conclusions again," he accused, frowning deeply at her. "Becky knows nothing of our relationship because I haven't said anything to her or anyone else about us. If she knows anything, it'd be from gossip, not me. I've been trying to preserve your privacy—our privacy." He leaned hard on the post. "When I asked her to call that morning, she wouldn't have known what kind of a meeting we were having. It seems plausible for her to guess it to be an appointment."

Lauren had to agree this might be true. "And tonight's conversation?" she asked, lifting one eyebrow slightly. "You told her you were with a client. That's hardly letting her come to her own conclusions."

He looked doubtful. "I don't recall telling her where I was or who I was with."

"But I heard you!" she insisted, gently rubbing away at the increasingly noticeable ache in her right arm. "I wasn't trying to listen in, but I couldn't help but overhear." A sad quality overtook her voice. "I truly wish I hadn't!"

A strange look flickered in his eyes. "I'm trying my best to figure this one out." His weight shifted from one foot to the other in thought. "I don't know how a call about thermostat covers comes even close to my calling you a client."

Curiosity got the better of her. "Thermostat covers?"

"I had locks put on the thermostat covers at the office this week," he explained. "It's one of those inherent gender difference problems. The guys keep turning the air conditioning up, and the gals keep turning it down. It was driving me absolutely crazy, so I had automatic thermostats installed and locked covers put over them." He rubbed a hand across his jaw. "But I'd forgotten about Ina from the cleaning service. She likes the air on full blast while she's working, and she called Becky when she couldn't open the cover." His eyes clouded in deliberation. "I remember telling Becky that Bill Anderson could have handled the call. He would have known to tell Ina the climate control. . ." The sentenced dropped off into nothing, the still night snatching the unsaid words.

Lauren's eyes widen with intense interest. "What?"

Jason didn't answer right away. Instead she could hear his laughter, softly at first and then more audible.

"What?"

"You don't get it?"

Her brow wrinkled in consideration, annoyance slowly creeping in. "Get what?"

"How the mix-up occurred!"

"No!" Nothing struck an answering chord.

"Do the words 'Ina the climate' mean anything to you?"

Lauren's eyes squinted in thought. "Ina the climate?"

"That's evidently what you mistook for 'I'm with a client,' " he reasoned. "Although I do have to say it couldn't have been done without a good deal of slurring and a drawl."

She looked up at Jason worriedly, thinking over his words. His explanation seemed exasperatingly possible, and much more than that—probable. All indications pointed to her own guilt and stupidity. She paused long and hard before speaking. "It seems I owe you an apology."

He dropped onto the step beside her. "Yes, you do!"

Something about the way he said the words made her pause again. She studied his face as he calmly waited. His hard expression had faded, replaced by an unreadable look. "Jason, I. . ." The words stuck in her throat. "I'm really sorry. I—accused you unjustly."

Jason took her hand in his. "Apology accepted." His steady gaze fixed her. "And this is where the rubber meets the road, so to speak."

Apprehension filled her. "What do you mean?"

"What I mean is, real forgiveness means total amnesty," he replied. "No-holds-barred amnesty." The sigh accompanying those words made Lauren wince. "Although our memories can't really forget the way we've been mistreated, how I was wrongly accused tonight or how badly I treated you five years ago, we do have control over how those memories are used. As far as I'm concerned, what happened tonight," he paused and snapped his fingers, "it's gone. I don't plan to discuss it again or ever use it against you, no matter the circumstances."

"Total forgiveness?"

He nodded. "Total forgiveness!"

"Just like Jesus," she added, her voice barely a whisper. The thought nudged her heart with guilt. How many times had she claimed forgiveness for Jason, only to bring his past shortcomings to the surface, letting it gasp for air before taking a dive under again? God's forgiveness wasn't anything like that, and He didn't tolerate it among His children. And the sins God had forgiven her were mountainous in contrast.

She felt Jason stir slightly beside her as he said, "I've given you my forgiveness freely. Now I want your forgiveness,

Lauren—real forgiveness this time. The problem tonight stemmed directly from your unwillingness to forgive what happened five years ago. You're still waiting for the other shoe to drop. I want a clean slate!"

Night sounds grew louder as tree frogs chorused together in the darkness. Lauren wrinkled her forehead in thought. Of course, she must forgive Jason and with true forgiveness, a total pardon. God wouldn't honor anything less.

"Jason," she spoke, her voice full of emotion. "I do forgive you and promise to file away those memories permanently." She paused. "And I'll try, with everything in me, to not let the past influence our today."

Jason stood and pulled her to her feet, looking into her face in a way surely meant to melt her heart. "You don't know what that means to me." He drew her close to his chest, gently cushioning her sling. "I know you must be awfully exhausted after last night and the hospital trip this morning, but I need to know one more thing."

Lauren drew back slightly to see his face. "What's that?"

"Are you willing to give God the chance to show us what He wants?"

"You mean about my staying the summer, don't you?" she asked, her voice trembling slightly.

"Yes."

She drew back completely to fully view him. "I need to know something before I can even begin to contemplate the possibility."

"Anything!"

"Are you in any way committed to someone else?" she asked bluntly. If he wasn't free, there was no use pursuing their relationship further. She didn't want a repeat of their last love story—it'd be like watching a bad film through for a second time.

Jason gave her a considering look before answering. "I'm a perfectly free man!" A smile crept over his face. "Is that all you needed to know?"

"And Becky?" She needed total assurance.

"Becky?" He looked perplexed for a moment before smiling again. "Becky's my secretary—nothing more! There's never been anything between Becky and me. Scout's honor!" He held up two fingers.

"It's three," Lauren said.

"What?"

"Three fingers—that is if you were a Boy Scout. Cub Scouts use two." Lauren drew his third finger up.

"Don't change the subject. And you?"

"Me?"

"Yes, you! While we're playing truth or dare, I'd like to ask you the same question. Are you committed in any way to Tom or anyone else?"

Sadness tugged at her again at the thought of Tom. Tomorrow he'd be gone from her life for good. "No."

"Then you'll stay the summer?"

There was a slight pause and a cautious answer. "Maybe!" She gave a sigh. "But it's not up to just me. I have a job to consider, an apartment standing empty, church duties—"

Gently he laid a finger to her lips. "All these things can be dealt with. Do you trust me enough to let me handle them?"

"You?"

"Yes, me!"

Lauren thought a moment, not sure what to say. She loved Jason and knew he was quite capable of getting his way when put to task. Even her employer might bend to his will. "All right, Jason. If God enables you to work things out, I'll stay the summer."

"That's all I needed to hear." Jason's eyes danced a jig. "And you, young lady, need to head up those steps and get your beauty sleep. It's been a long day for the both of us."

Lauren looked anxiously toward the dark cabin and instinctively cradled her good hand under the sling.

Jason followed her gaze perceptively. "It's all right! I'm going to be right outside the door all night long. You'll be quite safe."

"Tilly insisted I spend the night at her place. You can stay in the cabin. I don't think I can make up a bed for you, though," she stated with concern.

"Not to worry," he assured. "I've come prepared with a sleeping bag." He laughed at her whimsical look. "When you're ready, I'll walk you to Tilly's. Now up the steps."

Lauren yielded to his touch as he guided her toward the deck. She waited as he entered the cottage, giving it a through search before he'd allow her to enter.

"Everything's in dandy shape," he announced at last.

"Thank you, Jason." Instinctively she drew her hand to her throat, immediately remembering her missing necklace. "Did you talk with Larry about my necklace?"

A worried expression crossed his face. "Yes, I did. The cross necklace wasn't on the boy."

"It's lost again?" she noted in despair.

Jason drew an arm around her, his face close. "We'll find it. The boy must have dropped it somewhere here at the cottage or on the trail to Tilly's. We'll look for it tomorrow."

"Tomorrow's the Skipper's Festival," she reminded. "You won't have time."

"There's plenty of time." He moved her to the door. "You just get your things and let me worry about everything else." Lauren felt sure he was going to kiss her, but he drew away.

Lauren closed the screen, leaving the main door open. Finally, she collected her things. Glancing out the window, she watched Jason pull a dark sleeping bag from the trunk of his car.

# eighteen

Lauren awoke suddenly, opening startled eyes as she lifted her head from the pillow. Sunlight flooded the bedroom floor through the small window, and she quickly turned toward the bedside clock. Ten-thirty! The late hour quickly brought her to a sitting position. How could Tilly have let her sleep so long? Hastily she threw aside the covers and raced to the window, cupping the heavy, white cast as she did.

A satisfied smile slowly spread across her face. For once she relaxed in the knowledge of Jason's nearness. It felt so right! She dressed quickly, then grabbed her blue fleece jacket, carefully wove the cast through the loose arm opening, and headed for the hallway. Very much to her surprise, she felt refreshed.

Tilly had left a note on the kitchen table saying she had an errand to run before she headed for the Skipper's Festival, so Lauren gathered her things and left, locking the door securely behind her.

&

Inside her cabin, the aroma of coffee greeted her, and she quickly glanced about. An empty cup sat next to the coffeemaker and a half-filled carafe remained seated on the hot plate. Lauren drifted noiselessly back to the screen door and peered out. She hadn't seen Jason when she arrived, but now she noticed him crouched close to the deck floor on the far right, his back to her. Her eyes opened with the mildest flicker of interest as she watched his hand sweep back and forth across the deep gouges caused by the patio furniture during her unfortunate fall. His gaze seemed to intensify as he leaned closer. Then, as if sensing her presence, he slowly turned and met her stare. His face creased into smiles as he stretched up to his full height.

"Good morning," he greeted. "You're looking much better."

Lauren didn't know how he could judge through the hazy screen, but she took the compliment to heart anyway. "Good morning," she returned, taking note of his fresh clothes. "Have you been home this morning?" Even as she said it, the word home struck a peculiar chord. His home was really her house—the one unanswered question yet to be addressed.

"Nope!" He seemed to find amusement in her confusion. "I didn't think you'd mind me using your facilities. It's the least one could offer a man willing to risk his life guarding her home."

"I suppose," she said with mock indignation, leaning casually on the doorjamb. "And good help is so hard to come by these days. Guess I'll have to keep you happy with occasional perks."

His eyes twinkled. "And don't you forget it."

Lauren's eyes widened slightly, and she smiled at him. "Would it be too much to ask the help to fix some breakfast?" She chuckled, adding, "Or brunch—or whatever people have when they don't get up until the day's nearly half spent."

"That'll be extra, I'm afraid."

"Oh, really?"

"Of course." One brow rose upward into the blond thatch over his forehead, an impish light making his eyes gleam. "Especially if you want any more salon treatments."

Lauren blushed slightly. "I don't think that will be necessary."

He laughed and opened the screen door. "Go and get yourself ready for the day then. The Skipper's Festival starts this afternoon, and you don't want to miss my performance for sure." When she didn't move right away, he prodded her forward. "Hurry up, now, or you'll be even later than late getting your medicine."

Slowly Lauren made her way to the back hall, reluctant to break away from Jason. The feeling of freedom she felt with him seemed so novel, like a new toy one didn't want to part with. She hadn't realized the burden unforgiveness had placed on her heart for the past five years, not until it was lifted. Even the air seemed easier to breathe. A tickle of anticipation coursed through her. God had something wonderful ahead, she just knew.

A cool bath, fully brushed hair, and fresh clothes did wonders for her morale. The hard tasks of yesterday seemed easier today, something she attributed to her rested condition.

"Need help with the sling?" Jason asked, watching her adjust the blue folds without success as she entered the kitchen.

Lauren tried to move the back knot to one side. "It's making my neck hurt this morning."

"Let's see." Jason lifted the material slightly, examining her neck. "I can see why! The sling's rubbed a sore." She could feel his warm fingers move across the sling and the weight shift to the other side of her neck. "A bandage should fix the problem. Do you have any first aid supplies?" Lauren nodded, explaining their whereabouts, and a moment later Jason returned with the white box.

He gently applied an antiseptic and soft covering. "Better?"

"Much." She threw him a mischievous smile. "You're not only a good security guy, cook, hairstylist, and overall handyman, but you provide nursing care as well. Quite talented, I'd say."

Filling her cup with hot coffee, he motioned for her to sit. "I only need to win the Skipper's title today to make complete the set then, eh?" Lauren could see the amusement behind his serious gaze. He sat opposite her, his left ankle resting on his right knee as he quietly sipped his own coffee. "I spoke with Paul Waggoner earlier this morning."

Lauren's head snapped up to meet his gaze, the movement almost spilling her coffee. "You talked with my boss?" She didn't quite know what to expect from Jason's announcement the night before about taking care of things back in Cincinnati, but she hadn't quite expected this.

"He's a pretty nice guy," Jason answered back, nonplussed. "But you were right. He doesn't seem so inclined to let you go for the summer. I think he wants you back, broken arm and all."

Lauren's heart plunged straight to the floor. "Oh." Hadn't she told herself things weren't as simple as Jason presented? Yet she couldn't deny the disappointment all the same.

"Not to worry," Jason said with a shrug, watching her closely. There was total nonchalance in his voice. "I'm not multitalented for just any reason. This is only round one."

Lauren couldn't be so confident, but she said nothing.

"Hurry up and eat," he teased, "or we'll miss the festival."

❧

The Skipper's Festival was crowded. Hoots and screams of delight filled the air as Jason and Lauren passed through the midway.

"Can't interest you in riding the roller coaster, can I?" he asked, half laughing and pointing to the four-person car swooping down at an alarming rate along the steep rails. He squeezed her fingers in shameless teasing.

"You know very well I'd faint on the first drop." She laughed.

He smiled down at her. "Guess we'll have to stay with tamer activities. How about some midway games?"

Lauren nodded in agreement. Jason seemed different, more carefree. Had he experienced the same release of guilt and emotions she had? This emancipation was so new, she hardly knew how to handle it.

For an hour, Jason dragged Lauren by the hand from booth to booth. Twice he'd won unusable souvenirs by knocking down stacked milk cans and making baskets through small hoops. Finally, he seemed to tire of the games and went in search of the food booths.

"What's your pleasure?" he asked as they surveyed the line of vendors.

Lauren smiled and grabbed his hand, pulling him forward. "It looks like McDuffy's stand is here this year."

"Should have guessed," he laughed, easily following her lead. "You never could resist their corn dogs, eating more than any other girl could ever hope to."

She playfully slapped at his arm. "You love their corn dogs as much as I do, and you know it," she told him, stopping at the open serving window.

Jason only laughed and motioned the woman for two foot-long corn dogs. "I haven't had one of these in years."

"Then you're due!"

"I'm due for a lot of things after five years," he said, throwing Lauren a meaningful glance. His eyes sparkled, and she found herself holding his gaze.

"Your change, Sir," interrupted the woman, handing Jason his money and then two perfectly browned corn dogs.

Jason laced each with a stripe of mustard before happily handing one to Lauren. "Let's sit over there," he instructed, guiding her to an empty bench.

"These are wonderful," Lauren gushed, then took a second bite.

He laughed. "I must say you're right. I'd nearly forgotten."

"Told you so," she cried triumphantly.

Lauren couldn't believe the completeness she felt at Jason's side. Like old times, she assumed her starry-eyed role, but with totally new features and directions. Jason and Lauren were together again. A week ago she wouldn't have believed it possible.

"Come on," Jason urged, snapping her from a state of reverie just as she'd swallowed her last bite. "It's time for me to sign in." He led her to the registration table at the edge of the sandy beach, giving her a contagious smile. "Find me a couple of skipping stones, will you, while I fill out this paperwork?"

"You don't have your stones picked out yet?" she asked incredulously.

"Nope," he answered with a laugh. "Always pick them out just before the contest."

She pulled a face at him. "No wonder you never win."

He only chuckled. "Just find me a lucky stone."

Lauren did as bidden, carefully stooping and scouring the sand with one hand. She examined and discarded several stones.

"Got it!" she announced just as Jason joined her, proudly displaying the perfectly flat rock before him.

Jason scrutinized the stone she laid in his hand and gave her a nod of approval. "This year I'll win for sure," he declared.

"If you say so," Lauren teased. She watched as Jason concentrated on the stone, tumbling it over and over again with his fingers as if memorizing each facet.

The loud squawk of a bullhorn interrupted her thoughts. The skipping competition was about to begin.

"You'll cheer me on, won't you?" he asked.

"Of course. I'm your biggest fan."

He reached over and took her hand, raising it briefly to his lips. "I'm holding you to that."

Lauren could feel herself color. "Just make sure you skip that rock like it's never been skipped before."

Jason let her hand drop after a brief squeeze and mingled in with the crowd. Twenty-two contestants drew their lottery and gathered in line. Jason was difficult to miss, even in a crowd, with his blond hair looking almost white in the brilliant sun. He'd evidently drawn next to last, the reigning three-year champion right before him, and an unknown behind.

"Nervous?" asked a teasing voice from behind.

Lauren turned to face Larry Newkirk, a smile immediately coming to her lips. It was then she saw his young female companion. "Hello, Larry," she greeted warmly. "And who's this with you?"

The fair-haired woman smiled engagingly as Larry made introductions. He looked at Lauren's arm. "I see you're doing okay."

"Yes," Lauren agreed. "Thanks to you. I never did get a chance to properly tell you how much I appreciated all your help. Who knows what would have. . ." She shuddered to think of it.

The young woman nodded. "Larry's very brave."

Larry only grinned. "All in the line of duty." Then his expression turned solemn. "Jason did tell you; I couldn't find your cross necklace."

Lauren nodded with a sad smile. "I suppose it wasn't meant for me to have after all."

"Ah, don't worry," he encouraged. "It'll turn up again."

"Sure." Yet she knew it wouldn't happen.

Larry and his date soon wandered off, and Lauren immediately turned her attention back to the contest. She watched in anxious anticipation as each competitor stepped up to the line to throw his or her stone, some far, some miserably short. Halfway through, she saw Tilly and waved her over.

"I see Jason's got himself almost dead last," Tilly said cheerfully, her broad, plump face full of smiles. "That'll give the other chaps something to worry about."

Lauren chuckled. "What about the woman contestant?"

"What!" Tilly instantly scrutinized the group, her brows scrunched into wrinkles. "Well, if that don't beat all. That'll be a first." She snorted. "It'll do the boys good to have some real competition for a change."

"Yes, but we're rooting for Jason, remember," Lauren playfully rebuked.

"Of course, Girl. Who else!" She eyed Lauren closely. "I take it to mean things are patched."

Lauren nodded, finding it hard to keep from smiling.

"That's the way it should be." Tilly watched the next contestant complete his throw before speaking again. "I saw your Tom off to the ferry this mornin'."

Lauren slowly nodded again, remembering the errand Tilly mentioned in her note. "I appreciate your taking care of him." Although his inevitable departure caused sadness, she'd made the right choice. It was Jason she loved. She'd been in danger of mistaking loneliness for something deeper with Tom. "Did he seem okay?"

"He'll be right as rain soon enough," the older woman assured.

Both women shifted their attention as the reigning champion stepped up to the line. Silence fell among the multitude. Seconds seemed to drag before the stone finally took flight.

"Forty-three skips," announced the record keeper. "New record!"

The crowd broke out in claps of excitement.

Now Jason stepped up to the line in the sand, and Lauren clenched her hands nervously together. A small prayer escaped her lips, immediately followed by a request of forgiveness for such a selfish petition. But it seemed important Jason should win—to win at something—anything.

"Come on, Jason," she whispered.

Tilly didn't say a word.

Jason closed his eyes briefly before rolling the stone carefully in his hand. Then he drew his arm back and threw the rock low and flat. The stone skimmed the water, tapping the surface lightly several times, hovering low, never sinking. Forty-one, forty-two, forty-three—Lauren held her breath—forty-four—forty-five!

The announcer barked over the speakers, "Forty-five! It's another record, folks!"

The crowd went wild, and Jason threw a victorious arm in the air. A knowing smile crossed his lips as his gaze locked with Lauren's for several seconds. Then the trancelike moment broke as he was forced to move on, letting the last contestant forward. She watched the tall, thin man step up to the line. A hush fell over the spectators once again as the man began his windup pitch, snapping the stone hard against the water. The rock went airborne, but immediately tumbled perilously on the water's surface, sinking deftly after only ten skips. The crowd exhaled a sympathetic coo for the man, but cheers heartily resumed again when Jason was announced winner.

Lauren nearly choked on her happiness, coming quite close to it as Tilly turned to her, squeezing what little breath she had left in a bear hug.

"It's enough to make an ol' woman cry, it is," she squealed, wiping her wide thumb under her eye.

"Go ahead and have a good cry, Tilly," Lauren laughed with unconcealed enjoyment. "You deserve it! We all do."

She watched as several well-wishers patted Jason on the back as he threaded his way through the crowd to her.

"Congratulations," Lauren yelled excitedly over the roar.

There was great delight in his voice as he hurried forward. "I'm the happiest man in the world, Lauren Wright!" He caught her by surprise as he scooped her up in his arms, planting a kiss firmly on her lips. The crowd hooted.

"Jason!" Her face had to be cherry-red. Had he gone stark-raving mad?

"What?" he shouted happily, giving her a catching smile.

Lauren looked aghast at the mob of watching faces and again at Jason. He was grinning down at her, his gray eyes slightly narrowed. She felt her face being tipped closer as he landed another kiss on her lips.

"Jason Levitte!" she exclaimed.

This brought more hoots and whistles from the onlookers.

Jason leaned close to her ear. "I've never been happier," he announced, the warmth tickling her ear. "And I'll not let you spoil it by ever leaving Bay Island again."

Lauren looked up in confusion. "What?"

"You'll find out soon enough," Jason told her obscurely, his dimple deepening with his widening smile. "I have plans—"

"Come on, Levitte," intruded a voice at the microphone. "Up to the podium."

"Don't go anywhere," Jason instructed before sprinting off to the platform.

Lauren moved her arm in a helpless little gesture. What had Jason meant? What plans? What had come over him?

Tilly only shrugged her shoulders, a silly smile transfixed on her face, evidently pleased beyond belief. "Whatever it is, I'm sure it's worth waiting for."

# nineteen

It seemed forever before Jason finished his acceptance speech and joined her again, this time with a trophy under his arm. Tilly had discreetly disappeared.

Lauren suddenly felt anxious. What had he meant about his plans? She would surely die of curiosity if the answer didn't come soon.

Jason lightly grasped her arm, and a smile spread across his face. "Let's go."

"Where to?"

"Your home!"

Distress spread over her. She hadn't quite expected to leave the festival for Piney Point just yet. What was the man up to? But Jason seemed oblivious to her quandary as he led her to the car, their footsteps deadened by the soft grass. He opened the trunk and threw the trophy haphazardly inside, then slammed the lid.

"Jason," she cried. "You'll bust the thing before you even have a chance to display it."

He opened her door. "It's only a trophy."

"Only a trophy!" she scolded as soon as he seated himself behind the wheel. "You've tried for I don't know how many years to win that precious trophy. What's gotten into you?"

"Shush and be still," he laughed, much to her disconcertment.

They traveled in silence as Lauren's mind continued to somersault. "You missed the turn, Jason," she announced when the car veered from the usual route.

"I know," Jason said calmly. "I'm taking you to the house." He turned to look at her. "It's time you knew the truth."

Lauren swallowed hard. Wasn't this what she'd wanted all along—to know the truth about her house? Then why was her heart screaming for him to turn back? Jason edged the car up the long drive and parked neatly in front of the large, white garage door. Quickly he hopped out and opened her door.

"This way," Jason instructed, guiding her around to the front porch. Slowly he swung the wide French doors open.

Lauren stepped gingerly inside the great hall, nearly gasping at the beauty she saw. It was exactly as she'd pictured, every mental image coming to life. Even the beautiful cherry woodwork and stately light fixtures were hauntingly familiar. Lauren ran her hand across the shiny banister and a lump formed in her throat. Jason wouldn't taunt her, would he? Not with her dream house.

"Jason." She nearly choked.

"Shush!" he whispered softly, letting one finger slide gently over her lips. "I want to show you the tower." He led her up the carpeted steps.

The tower door opened into a spaciously windowed room. The breathtaking view drew Lauren to the glass. "It's beautiful!"

"It's yours," Jason said, his voice so low she could barely catch it. "I made this tower, this house—for you." He stood beside her, looking out the large window toward the lighthouse in the distance.

"For me?" she asked, her voice but a bare whisper.

"I began building it after Tara confessed." He turned toward her, taking her hands in his. "When the truth of your innocence came out, I nearly died—from shame, from my stupidity. But then there was hope—hope you might come back, and hope you'd forgive me. I built this house—your house—on that hope."

"And then came Tara's phone call," Lauren finished sadly.

"Yes," Jason concurred, shaking his head. "The infamous phone call."

"But this tower," Lauren began after a moment's silence; "it was never part of the plan."

"No," he agreed. "I added it for me." He pointed toward the lighthouse. "It's to remind me, to keep me from forgetting that God's my lighthouse." His gray eyes deepened. "If

I'd kept my eyes on His light to begin with, you would have never been forced to leave Bay Island." Lauren sensed his raw pain. "When Tara made that call to you, it squeezed the last drop of hope from me. I knew then the house was a wasted effort; you were never coming back." He sighed. "But the house was nearly complete, so I finished it. Then everywhere I turned, the house kept reminding me of you, torturing me about what a hardened person I'd thought you'd become—what I'd made you become." A smile slowly crept over his face. "But God's told me there's a second chance for us."

Lauren drew her brows together in deliberation. "God told you that!"

He smiled again. "I asked God to show me. And He has!"

"How?" she asked warily.

"I asked God for a sign. If you were meant to stay with me, I'd win the tournament." The crooked smile deepened. "And I won! It was a sign."

"You asked God to do that?" Lauren cried, her own smile forming as she suddenly remembered her own little prayer.

"And I wouldn't ask—not ordinarily," Jason conceded. "But there was so little time, and I knew God's hand was in it." He smiled triumphantly. "I've never skipped a stone that far in my life. It had to be God's hand." But Lauren gave him a wary look. "And there's something else."

She drew in a deep breath. "Yes."

Jason reached into his back pocket and produced a white handkerchief. "I found something that belongs to you." Slowly he unwrapped the creased fold, finally revealing a glittering piece of jewelry.

Her eyes widened. "My necklace! But how—"

"I told you, God's hand was in it." Gently he lifted the delicate chain like an entranced cobra and slipped it around her neck, centering the cross. "It made sense to trace the path the thief took, and sure enough—"

"Where I fell?" She suddenly knew, recalling how Jason had examined the deck that morning.

"Actually," Jason began, "the necklace fell between the deck boards where he collided with you. He must have dropped it in the scuffle." He smiled. "It wasn't easy fishing it out, I can tell you."

"You didn't crawl under the deck did you?" she asked in horror. "There's poison ivy and snakes. . ." A shiver coursed down her spine.

He laughed easily. "No, I'm not that foolish. I fished it out through the deck boards with a hanger. Not an easy task, but doable."

"Oh, Jason," she murmured. "How can I ever thank you? Losing it again was nearly as unbearable as losing it the first time. Now, it's like a second chance for a second chance."

"And I believe in second chances." He drew his finger reflectively across her cheek. "I can't bear the thought of hurting you again, and I don't want to wreck the life you've finally built for yourself." He seemed to be struggling again. "But I love you, Lauren—I've never stopped, and I can't live my life without you."

Lauren's heart stepped up a beat. "You really love me?"

Immediately Jason embraced her. "Of course, I love you!" He looked down at her. "Is that so hard to believe?"

"Not anymore. It seems so real right now."

"I plan to spend my life convincing you just how real it is." Jason clasped her chin and drew her face close. Their lips met. "Now what do you say?"

Lauren smiled stupidly. "I say you need a shave, Jason Levitte."

Jason rubbed his jaw. "I already know that." He smirked. "What I want to know is what you think about us." His gaze held hers. "Is there an us?"

"Your methods of finding God's assurance and blessing for us is shaky—at best," Lauren teased. "But I do still love you, and I do believe in second chances too. And you know what?"

"What?" he whispered.

Lauren looked up smiling. "Since my boss won't let me have temporary time off, I'll just have to make it a permanent time off. Know of anyone looking for an accountant?"

He grinned. "Let me check around. I'm sure there's a suitable employer for you somewhere on the island." Drawing her close, he whispered, "You will stay, won't you?"

Lauren nodded. "I must warn you, though. God's not through with me. I still have a lot to work though—forgiving Tara, forgiving the church—"

"You're not alone," Jason replied, pulling her nearer still. "This time we'll work through the problems together, including my work schedule. We'll set the priorities straight—God first, then us—then work."

"Sounds good so far." Lauren nestled closer.

"Do you want to see the rest of your house, then?" He pulled her back just enough to see her face clearly.

"You mean our house, don't you?" she teased.

"Not just yet it isn't," Jason replied seriously. "But I plan to win your heart back, lock stock, and barrel. And when you finally say 'I do,' then it'll be our house."

"If you insist," Lauren razzed.

Jason answered her with a kiss. "I insist."

# A Letter To Our Readers

Dear Reader:

In order that we might better contribute to your reading enjoyment, we would appreciate your taking a few minutes to respond to the following questions. We welcome your comments and read each form and letter we receive. When completed, please return to the following:

Fiction Editor
Heartsong Presents
PO Box 719
Uhrichsville, Ohio 44683

1. Did you enjoy reading *Bay Island* by Beth Loughner?
   ❑ Very much! I would like to see more books by this author!
   ❑ Moderately. I would have enjoyed it more if

   _____

   _____

   _____

2. Are you a member of **Heartsong Presents**?  ❑ Yes  ❑ No
   If no, where did you purchase this book? _____

   _____

3. How would you rate, on a scale from 1 (poor) to 5 (superior), the cover design? _____

4. On a scale from 1 (poor) to 10 (superior), please rate the following elements.

   ____ Heroine        ____ Plot
   ____ Hero           ____ Inspirational theme
   ____ Setting        ____ Secondary characters

5. These characters were special because?_____

_____

_____

6. How has this book inspired your life?_____

_____

_____

7. What settings would you like to see covered in future **Heartsong Presents** books? _____

_____

_____

8. What are some inspirational themes you would like to see treated in future books? _____

_____

_____

9. Would you be interested in reading other **Heartsong Presents** titles? ❏ Yes ❏ No

10. Please check your age range:

    ❏ Under 18        ❏ 18-24

    ❏ 25-34          ❏ 35-45

    ❏ 46-55          ❏ Over 55

Name_____

Occupation _____

Address _____

City_____ State_____ Zip_____

# Christmas Duty

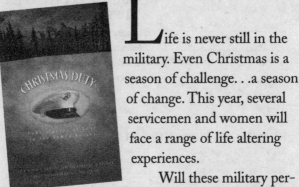

Life is never still in the military. Even Christmas is a season of challenge. . .a season of change. This year, several servicemen and women will face a range of life altering experiences.

Will these military personnel find Christmas to be a time of renewed hope? Will they hold on to their faith in the Christmas Child and the Savior who can guide their lives today?

Contemporary, paperback, 352 pages, 5 $\frac{3}{16}$" x 8"

# Heart♥song

# Presents

## Great Inspirational Romance at a Great Price!

**Heartsong Presents** books are inspirational romances in contemporary and historical settings, designed to give you an enjoyable, spirit-lifting reading experience. You can choose wonderfully written titles from some of today's best authors like Hannah Alexander, Andrea Boeshaar, Yvonne Lehman, Tracie Peterson, and many others.

*When ordering quantities less than twelve, above titles are $3.25 each.*
*Not all titles may be available at time of order.*

# ℋEARTSONG ♥ PRESENTS

# Love Stories
# Are Rated G!

That's for godly, gratifying, and of course, great! If you love a thrilling love story but don't appreciate the sordidness of some popular paperback romances, **Heartsong Presents** is for you. In fact, **Heartsong Presents** is the premiere inspirational romance book club featuring love stories where Christian faith is the primary ingredient in a marriage relationship.

Sign up today to receive your first set of four, never-before-published Christian romances. Send no money now; you will receive a bill with the first shipment. You may cancel at any time without obligation, and if you aren't completely satisfied with any selection, you may return the books for an immediate refund!

Imagine. . .four new romances every four weeks—two historical, two contemporary—with men and women like you who long to meet the one God has chosen as the love of their lives. . .all for the low price of $10.99 postpaid.

To join, simply complete the coupon below and mail to the address provided. **Heartsong Presents** romances are rated G for another reason: They'll arrive Godspeed!